WHEN WE FALL

A LODGE SERIES NOVEL

J.H. CROIX

DEDICATION

*To all those who face the medical curveballs life can throw our
way with bravery, humility and incredible strength.*

Sign up for my newsletter for information on new releases!
http://jhcroixauthor.com/subscribe/

Follow me!
jhcroix@jhcroix.com
https://amazon.com/author/jhcroix
https://www.bookbub.com/authors/j-h-croix
https://www.facebook.com/jhcroix
https://www.instagram.com/jhcroix/

CHAPTER 1

A rock came tumbling down the steep mountainside, bouncing off a tree as it hurtled down the partially wooded slope. Lacey Adams heard it and quickly glanced up to see it heading straight for her. She scrambled out of the way, only to lose her footing on the gravelly trail and crash to the ground onto her hip. "Oomph!"

"How's it going up there?" Quinn Haynes called out.

"Just fine!" Lacey called in reply, gritting her teeth against the sharp pain in her hip. She knew she'd be fine once she got back on her feet, so she didn't think it was worth the bother to whine about her fall. She waited until the boulder came to a thudding stop against a spruce tree at the bottom of the slope before pushing herself up on her hands. Once she was standing again, she took stock and figured she'd have a hell of a bruise on her hip when they got to camp tonight.

Otherwise, it was all in a day's work for her. She and Quinn were leading a guided photography trip in Katmai National Park, deep in the wilderness of Alaska. Katmai was renowned for its remote beauty and particularly for the brown bears that frequented the famed Katmai River Falls where remote video cameras recorded the massive bears feeding off salmon running through the river. Lacey had led several trips here over the years with the area popular for wilderness lovers. The falls were carefully managed with electric fences and viewing platforms positioned at safe distances, curbing the danger that normally came with being in such proximity to bears. They were many miles away from the river falls right now and trekking deep into the wilderness with a group of wildlife photographers committed to more pure forms of photography, namely capturing wildlife in more challenging circumstances than the convenient viewing platforms by the falls.

She'd volunteered to check this trail out before they took the group along this route to reach another mountain peak ahead. She'd confirmed what they suspected—the trail had been mostly washed out by the spring thaw when the melting snow turned into raging streams. The gravel here was loose, along with the rocks up above. If Lacey had her way, they'd take the slightly longer route through the trees. In her years of backcountry guiding, she'd learned it was usually wiser to go slow than to take potentially risky short-cuts. It was one thing to risk her own injury, another to risk that of her clients. She ran her own small business from Diamond Creek, Alaska and often paired with other guides she knew from her years of working in the wilds of Alaska. Quinn Haynes was an old friend and occasionally joined her on these trips. She hadn't seen him in over two years when they confirmed this trip. He'd taken a break from guiding to finish his medical degree. Now, he had a fancy title to go with living on the edge. He'd spent the last year overseas providing medical care in war torn regions.

Lacey carefully made her way back down the mountainside and met Quinn at the bottom where he was waiting. Their clients had taken a short hike to a nearby field to watch and wait for wildlife to pass by, hoping for anything from wild birds to moose to bears to give them a chance for some good photos. Quinn grinned when he saw her. "I'm guessing we won't be using that shortcut. You okay?"

She had a slight limp from her hip's collision with the rocky ground. She figured it would work itself out once they got moving again. The pain had dulled to an ache already. "I'm fine. The slope is rocky and loose. Let's take the longer way through the trees. Aside from not wanting anyone else to fall on their tail, I'd rather not worry about the expensive cameras they're hauling."

Quinn's amber hair glinted in the morning sun when he nodded. His eyes, almost a precise match with his hair, coasted over her. "You sure you're okay? You've got quite the limp."

Lacey sighed, slightly annoyed with his concern. "I'm fine. Give me a few minutes."

He turned to walk at her side when she reached him. They walked back toward the camp at a leisurely pace. Lacey's hip started to loosen as she'd predicted. By the time they arrived at camp, her limp had almost disappeared. Quinn strode to his tent and came out with a thermos.

"Coffee for you," he said as he handed it over with a grin.

Lacey plunked down in a camp chair and unscrewed the thermos lid. The coffee was plenty warm and dark. After a long swallow, she sighed and leaned back. "Thanks. I forgot you somehow manage to make the best coffee even when we're in the middle of nowhere."

Quinn chuckled and sat down across from her in another folding chair, his rangy form barely fitting in the chair. Lacey caught herself when her eyes began a slow investigation of Quinn. She didn't know what it was because she'd known Quinn for years, but ever since he'd met her at the start of this trip, she was uncomfortably aware of how handsome he was. He was in superb physical condition, rugged and fit, every inch of him honed muscle. His skin was bronzed from days living in the outdoors. He was a man who threw himself into whatever environment he happened to be in—whether it was the wilderness of Alaska, the beaches of a remote island, or the desert somewhere.

It wasn't that she hadn't noticed he was handsome before, but she'd never had any physical response to him until this trip. The last few days had been downright annoying for her. If she had a few spare minutes and he was nearby, he was like a magnet for her eyes and her body hummed with a buzz of awareness. She mentally shook herself and lifted her eyes above the trees. It was early fall, yet still quite warm for Alaska. The sun was up, brightening the snow-covered mountain peaks of the Aleutian Range. Conveniently, the wilderness gave her plenty to stare at other than Quinn.

They sat in the quiet with nothing other than the sound of water sliding over rocks in the background. A stream was close to their camp, offering a place to bathe and easy water access for drinking and cooking. They had two more nights here before they hiked out.

Later that afternoon, Lacey was leading the way back from their hike when both of her knees buckled suddenly. Weakness like she'd never felt before crashed through her body. She stumbled sideways and gripped a tree to steady herself. She was startled at the feeling, but steeled herself to will it away. After several deep breaths, she felt almost normal, so she pushed off the tree and began walking again. She glanced behind her to see Quinn had stopped with their group and was pointing at something in the distance. He was a veritable font of information about the geology of Alaska, so he was an extra plus as far as customers were concerned. She breathed a sigh of relief because it didn't appear any of them had noticed her stumble.

That night after the four photographers had retired to their tents, she glanced over at hers and sighed. Sometime during the hike away from camp, some type of animal, likely a marmot, had shredded a corner of the tent door, just enough to tear the fastener to the tent pole. Now, the tent leaned drunkenly to one side. That meant she would be sharing Quinn's tent tonight. Not such a great plan if her body's reaction to the idea told her anything. The moment she'd heard Quinn chuckle and comment she'd be sleeping with him tonight, heat had rolled through her body in a flash. She needed to get over this weird attraction to him as soon as possible. She didn't really do the whole relationship thing—too messy, too inconvenient. She'd also found that men tended to shy away from her anyway. She was too much of a tomboy.

She'd temporarily considered just sleeping outside under the stars, but that wasn't smart. Autumn nights were cold out in the wilderness and while a tent didn't offer too much protection, it was better than nothing. She looked across the dying fire to Quinn. His features were shadowed in the dim light, his amber hair gilded with gold in the flickering firelight. He glanced up and caught her eyes. For a flash, she thought she saw something in his gaze, but he shuttered it and his usual teasing smile hooked the corners of his mouth.

"I'm about to crash. You want me to help drag your sleeping bag in the tent?"

She stood swiftly. "Nah. I got it. Mind putting the fire to bed while I do that?"

She heard him stand as she strode toward her torn tent. She gathered her sleeping bag and carefully tidied up her backpack before carrying everything over to Quinn's tent. He was using a stick to sift through the coals and push them down into the pile of ash. Moments later, she was kneeling over trying to straighten out her sleeping bag when she heard the tent zipper. She scrambled to turn around. In her rush, she found herself a mere inch or so from his face. For a beat, she wanted to close the space and see if his lips felt as good as they looked—full and sensual against his strong and masculine features.

Instead she scrambled back with her heart beating staccato in her chest and that inconvenient desire flooding her. Quinn merely grinned and crawled into the tent beside her. Without a word, he yanked his t-shirt off and slipped into his sleeping bag.

"G'night," he said, his voice gruff.

She could hear the smile in his voice because that's how he always was. Everything held a hint of fun for him. Meanwhile, he'd left her dry-mouthed and nearly panting at the glimpse of his chest—all sculpted muscle and a true six-pack of abs. She'd seen him shirtless before, but she'd never thought much of it. What the hell was wrong with her? She shook her head and slipped into her own sleeping bag, grateful she'd be cocooned away from his body through the night.

She woke hours later, her hand—oh my god!—her hand was sliding over the hard planes of his chest. While somehow, her tank top had slid up and she was draped over him, one of her bare breasts pressing against his side and his hand cupping her bottom. She had absolutely no idea how they ended up tangled together like this, but both of their sleeping bags were unzipped and one of her legs was thrown over his. It felt *sooo* good to be close to him like this, her body was nearly aflame with need. This was not good, definitely not good.

* * *

QUINN CAME to slowly and realized he was rock hard with need and Lacey was draped all over him. He felt her lush bottom under his palm and almost groaned at how good it felt. Lacey Adams had been forbidden fruit for as long as he'd known her. She was always all business when she was around him, so he'd done his best to snuff out his body's reaction to her. Lacey was a good friend, and he respected her completely. She was a strong woman through and through, and he valued their friendship. He'd tucked his desire away, even though it occasionally made itself known anyway. But he couldn't help himself from appreciating how damn tempting she was with her auburn hair, her bright green eyes, and her body, which was nothing short of a work of art. She was completely fit. Her life demanded it with her years of leading hikes, dog sledding trips, cross-country skiing and then some in the wilderness. Somehow though, she retained her femininity with an hourglass figure, lush breasts and generous hips to soften her athletic build.

To wake with her like this sent his body and mind into all kinds of wild imaginings. Suddenly she stiffened against him. Ah hell, she was awake and now he had to find a way to be a gentleman about this. Because unless she made it crystal clear she wanted something more, he'd try to respect their friendship. Her hand stilled on his chest and she slowly lifted her head.

"Um, I'm not sure how this happened," she said, her words rough with sleep.

Seeing as he knew damn well she could feel his hard cock against the leg she'd thrown across him, he couldn't really deny his state. He chuckled. "Me neither."

Her eyes lifted and met his in the dark. He'd give anything for just enough light to be able to read her gaze. With his pulse thundering and lust lashing at him, he held his breath and willed his body under control.

She shifted her leg off of him. The feel of her silky skin sliding over his only served to tighten the need clawing at him. She slowly untangled herself from him, and he reluctantly let his hands ease off of her. She sat up and tugged her tank top down and looked over at him again. "Didn't mean to climb all over you like that," she said, her tone sheepish.

He aimed for nonchalant. "No need to apologize. We were asleep." He left unsaid the fact he would have happily allowed her to climb all over him again, but he sensed he needed to bide his time if he was ever to have a chance with Lacey.

She was quiet for several beats before she spun around and slipped back inside her sleeping bag. "Right, we were sleeping," she said softly.

He listened to the sound of her breathing as she drifted back into sleep. He lay in the dark, wide-awake as his body settled down. The hot lust surging through him gradually ebbed away. His mind tumbled with questions, wondering if the response he sensed from her was genuine, or his own wishful thinking. An owl called in the trees nearby with another owl returning the call from a distance. He finally managed to fall back into a light sleep.

The following morning, Quinn woke before Lacey. He rolled his head to the side, a smile curling at the sight of her. Her auburn hair lay in a tousle around her face and shoulders. She was on her side facing him with her hands tucked under her chin. Her full lips were relaxed and tiny freckles were scattered across the bridge of her nose and cheeks. He resisted the urge to lean over and kiss her. As if she sensed him looking at her, her eyes opened, green with flecks of gold and bright in the gray light of dawn.

"Morning," he said.

She shifted onto her back and stretched before rolling to face him again. "Good morning. How long have you been awake?"

"Just a few minutes."

"How's your hip?"

She moved her legs and shrugged one shoulder. "A little sore, but that's all."

She pushed up on one hand and crossed her legs under her. Her hair draped around her shoulders, long waves falling around the curves of her breasts, which were inconveniently on display in her fitted tank top. She leaned over and dug around in her backpack, tugging out a flannel button-down shirt, which she threw over her shoulders. He watched while she shimmied into a pair of fleece leggings. She glanced over her shoulder as she slid her feet into a pair of lightweight boots. "Don't suppose you'll be making coffee this morning?"

He grinned. "No need to ask."

She returned his grin and unzipped the tent flap, disappearing through it. He dug through his own backpack and tugged out another set of clothes. Moments later, he was lacing up his boots when he heard a shuffling sound and then a thump. Lacey's sharp cry was distinct. He scrambled out of the tent to find her on the ground by the blackened fire circle.

Peter and Chad, two of the photographers on the trip with them, were nearby. Chad was leaning over beside Lacey. "You okay?" he asked.

Quinn raced to Lacey's side, kneeling down. "What happened?" He tried to keep the alarm out of his voice.

Lacey had fallen in a tangle, her legs crossed at the ankles. She started to move, all but swatting Chad and Quinn away, but her hand flopped on the ground. Quinn eased an arm around her back, propping her weight against him. "Easy. Tell me what happened."

Lacey shook her head. "I can't see well. Everything's all blurry."

Chad caught his eyes. "She said a minute ago that her legs felt tired and then all of a sudden she collapsed."

Quinn's doctor brain switched on and he started rifling through possibilities right away. Given her slip yesterday, it could be related solely to that, or it could be something else. Right now, he needed to get her comfortable.

"Let's get you over to one of the chairs." He and Chad slowly eased her up.

He could sense her irritation. The fact she didn't shove them away and stand on her own concerned him. Once she was seated in a camp chair, he stood and glanced around. "Can you grab me that water bottle?" he asked, gesturing to Peter who'd been waiting nearby while he and Chad had helped Lacey to the chair.

Peter snagged the water bottle in question and strode in his direction. Quinn met him on the way. "Notice anything before she fell?" he asked, his voice low.

"Not much more than what Chad said. She mentioned her legs felt tired. Before that, she seemed, I don't know, kind of out of it. Just for a minute or so and then she fell."

Quinn nodded as he took the proffered water bottle from Peter, his worry increasing. "Thanks. We'll give her a few to see if she's feeling better. Hope you guys don't mind."

Peter's eyes widened. "Of course not! You've already given us the best trip we've ever had. We're happy to sit tight as long as we need. Don't even worry about it."

"Good to know. Let me see how she's doing."

Quinn headed back to Lacey's side, hooking his hand around a camp chair on the way over and setting it down beside her. "Have some water," he said, handing her the bottle.

She curled her hand around the bottle and took a long swallow. After she lowered it, he noticed her grip was shaky, so he reached over and took it from her. "How you feeling now?"

She canted her eyes to his and he saw fear in their depths, such an unusual feeling for Lacey, his worry notched higher. "Weird. I feel weird," she finally said. "After I came out of the tent, I just started to feel funny. One of my legs felt numb and both of them felt weak. For a second, I couldn't see right and then I just fell. That blurry thing is gone and my legs are starting to feel more normal, but it's just weird. What the hell happened?"

Quinn's mind flipped through possibilities, but he didn't want to go there right now with her. What she described could be minor, or not. The foreboding 'or not' wouldn't be a helpful place for him to explore just now. "Maybe your fall yesterday was a little harder than you thought. Let's see how you feel after a little bit. You still up for coffee?"

She grinned and nodded emphatically. "That might be just what I need."

* * *

Two days later, Lacey made her way along the gravel path leading to the airstrip that would fly them out of Katmai and back to Anchorage. After her odd episode the other morning, she'd had some of Quinn's coffee and felt like herself after that. The rest of the trip had been uneventful. Well, they'd had a close encounter with a brown bear and breathed a sigh of relief after they avoided two mama moose and their calves, but that was part of hiking in the wilderness in Alaska. Quinn was taking up the rear as they made their way to the airstrip. She could hear the whirr of the plane's prop in the distance. She glanced skyward and suddenly her vision blurred again. She stopped right where she was and shook her head. Just like the other day, her legs felt weak and one of them started tingling. "No, no, no, no," she mumbled to herself. She must have looked up too quickly. That's probably what happened the other morning. She ignored the weakness and tingling and started walking again. Her right leg wouldn't cooperate. She felt as if she was dragging it behind her. On sheer will alone, she kept trudging along the path.

Before she knew it, Quinn was at her side, catching her as she fell, his hold so strong and sure. She just let go because she couldn't hold herself up anymore. The last thing she remembered were Quinn's amber eyes locking onto hers. "You're okay. I've got you."

CHAPTER 2

The whirr of the small plane's prop drowned out Quinn's voice. Lacey kept her eyes closed, hoping she could pick up enough pieces of whatever he was saying. She wondered how close they were to Anchorage.

"...could be a few options...she said she didn't hit her head when she fell the other day...rather not speculate..."

After accepting all she could hear were bits and pieces, she gave up and opened her eyes. She was resting across three of the six seats in the plane. After years of complaining about the cramped space on the small planes that flew over the wilderness of Alaska, she finally got to stretch out all because she'd collapsed. She'd rather be jammed into one of the tiny seats if it meant she could erase the odd episodes she'd experienced over the last few days. She pushed up onto her elbows and looked around. Quinn and Chad were seated on the floor of the plane while the other three photographers were crammed into the remaining seats.

Quinn was facing her, his hands clasped in front of his bent knees. His eyes caught hers, concerned and assessing.

"How you feeling?" he asked, as he rolled onto his feet and carefully stood, slipping past Chad who scooted over to make room in the cramped space.

Lacey rolled her eyes. "You don't have to come rushing over here. I'm only three feet away."

Quinn chuckled as he sat on the floor beside her row of seats, leaning against the side of the plane. "Would it kill you to accept someone worrying about you?"

She pushed up a little further and slid her back up against the plane. "It wouldn't kill me, but it annoys the hell out of me," she said with a sigh. She mentally ran a check to assess how she felt. Once again, she felt fine. She had no idea why she was having these strange episodes of weakness, but she knew she didn't like it. At all. She caught Quinn's eyes. "Any idea what's going on with me?"

She saw a flash of something in Quinn's eyes. He was quiet for a long moment before he finally spoke. "It's not going to help for me to speculate. Let's get you to the hospital when we land and get you checked out. You sure you didn't hit your head when you fell the other day?"

"I'm sure! I swear. I fell on my hip and that's it. How could I hit my head and not notice anyway? So if it's not that, what the hell is it?"

Quinn shrugged. "I'm not trying to piss you off by asking if you hit your head. If you did, it might explain a few things. If not, well, let's leave it to a doctor."

"You are a doctor!"

His low chuckle came again, sending a soft shiver through her. Here she was, just coming to after passing out in his arms, a most definitely *not* sexy moment, and somehow this inconvenient attraction to Quinn kept popping up and surprising her. She mentally shook herself and threw a glare at him.

"Maybe so, but I'm not your doctor."

"Yeah, but can't you give me a few ideas? You got your

medical degree at Harvard. Surely you have some thoughts about it." She was relieved to be feeling normal again, but scared inside about the weakness she'd experienced. She wanted answers and wanted them now.

Quinn held her eyes for several beats, his amber gaze concerned and somber. "Lace, there are so many things that could be going on. It's not worth it to guess until you can get a check up and they can run a few tests. Weakness and numbness can be as simple as a misalignment in your spine. I'm sure you're freaking out in your head, but don't make it more than it is."

Lacey took a deep breath and let it out with a sigh, closing her eyes and swallowing against the worry tightening her throat. She'd always prided herself on being healthy, fit and strong. She did *not* like wondering why she'd collapsed twice and only escaped collapsing another time because a tree happened to be right beside her. She wanted to believe it was as simple as needing a spinal adjustment, but something told her that wasn't the case. Opening her eyes, she found Quinn's warm amber gaze on her. Part of her wanted to allow herself to savor his concern, while another part of her chafed against it. She'd never depended on any man and certainly didn't want to start doing it now. Most definitely not when she couldn't make heads or tails of her out of the blue attraction to Quinn.

The last time she'd seen him, she'd felt nothing other than warm camaraderie with him. He was a good friend whom she saw every so often on trips when they both worked for the same wilderness guiding business in Anchorage. Three years ago, he'd returned to Harvard to finish his medical degree and residency overseas after that. He came back to Alaska this year. When he'd offered via email to run this trip with her, she'd been excited. Quinn was easy to work with and she looked forward to seeing him. He'd stepped off the plane in Anchorage, and her body hummed at the sight of him. To make matters worse, she felt vulnerable and out of sorts that he'd gone and saved her from falling on her face on the way to the plane.

He angled his head to the side. "Stop worrying yourself when you don't even know what to worry about."

Good thing he couldn't know she wasn't just worrying about what was wrong with her, but her body's reaction to him. She aimed for nonchalant. "I'll try."

* * *

QUINN RESTED his elbow on a table in the examination room he'd stepped into to confer with the doctor. Quinn had met Dr. Julia Clark in passing, but he didn't know her well. She was no-nonsense with her short dark hair, brown eyes and narrow square glasses adding to the overall sense of a completely practical woman. She adjusted her white jacket and pushed her glasses up her nose when she looked over at Quinn.

"Lacey signed a release for me to talk with you, so I thought maybe you could give me an idea of how she'll handle what I'm about to tell her," Dr. Clark said.

"Is there a reason you're concerned?" Quinn countered. His worry for Lacey flared into full-blown dread. He feared Dr. Clark was about to confirm his suspicions.

Dr. Clark pursed her lips and sighed. "Look, I think you probably suspected what I do. We won't be able to know until she has another episode, but this looks like Multiple Sclerosis. The MRI shows a few brain lesions suggestive of MS. Right now, I'm only noting a single episode, but the MRI gives us a pretty strong clue. I don't doubt the findings, but I'm guessing your friend is most definitely not going to take this too well."

Quinn's chest tightened. Dr. Clark had said aloud the one diagnosis he'd hoped wouldn't be on the table. He'd meant what he said to Lacey when he'd said her symptoms could be a number of things, but in the back of his mind he'd worried about MS. While he knew many people lived with MS and managed it well, Dr. Clark was discerning enough to notice Lacey's tendency to rely on her strength. Even if she had MS and even if her MS was symptomatic sporadically with potentially years without symptoms, Lacey would chafe against it. That was only if she didn't have the misfortune of the more serious type of MS, which could lead to her being wheelchair bound eventually. He forcibly knocked his mind off considering that possibility. Quinn was startled at the depth of his reaction to how Lacey might feel about this, along with the level of concern he felt on her behalf. He was completely unprepared for the tightness around his heart. Lacey was all verve and strength. This possibility struck hard at that.

He looked over at Dr. Clark. "You're right about that. She won't be thrilled about any of this."

Dr. Clark nodded slowly. "Right then. Well, I'll go talk to her. Don't suppose you'd like to join me?"

Quinn pushed away from the counter. "If she's okay with it, sure. Just remember, she's my friend first, not a patient."

Only minutes later, Quinn watched Lacey from a few feet away. He shackled the urge to step to the side of the table where she sat and hug her. Her green eyes were wide and disbelieving. The tiny freckles scattered across her cheeks and nose stood out under the harsh fluorescent lights of the examining room. Her eyes flicked to him, to the floor and back to Dr. Clark.

"I don't understand. You're saying these, these stupid episodes might mean I have MS, but you're not giving me a diagnosis yet. You're saying it's a...what did you say?" Lacey asked, her tone exasperated.

"Clinically Isolated Syndrome, CIS. That's the diagnosis

when we don't have enough confirmation to say the disease is progressing. You may never have any other symptoms or episodes like this, in which case this will be a one-off episode. Or, you may experience other episodes. If, and that's a definite if, that happens, we'll run more tests and make a determination then."

Lacey swung one leg back and forth rapidly before she finally nodded. "Right. Okay then, so this is all one big maybe." She pushed off the table and rubbed her hands together. "Is there anything else before I go?"

Dr. Clark glanced to him, as if looking for help. He shrugged because he knew damn well now wasn't the time for more discussion. He had to forcibly hold himself back from pulling Lacey into his arms. A sense of protectiveness he'd never experienced washed over him. Dr. Clark looked back to Lacey, her expression soft. "No, nothing else. If you don't mind, I'd like to touch base with your doctor in Diamond Creek. If nothing else comes of this, it'll still be good for her to have the MRI results."

Lacey nodded jerkily. "Fine, fine. I think I already signed a release."

After a few more moments of stilted conversation while Dr. Clark confirmed she had a release on record, Quinn walked down the long hallway at the hospital with Lacey. Hours earlier, they'd landed in Anchorage and he'd driven straight here. She'd refused to call her family in Diamond Creek, insisting she'd get checked out only so she could prove to him all she needed was a chiropractic adjustment.

Lacey's arms were clutched around her waist while she all but stalked down the hall. She reached the revolving door that led outside. The door whooshed behind them as they stepped outside. Lacey strode quickly to the parking lot. She turned to face him when she reached his car. When he caught up, he stopped a few feet in front of her. Her eyes bounced to the ground and then back to him. She toed the pavement, idly kicking a rock. "So, I'm not due to fly back to Diamond Creek until tomorrow. Do you want to grab some dinner?"

This conversation probably would've happened regardless of this afternoon. Whenever they ran trips, they often had casual meals together. Quinn sensed Lacey needed him not to talk about the discussion she'd just had with Dr. Clark, but rather just do what they would usually do. As much as he wanted to somehow offer comfort, he gathered for now this was the only comfort she would accept. "Of course. Susitna Burgers & Brew?"

At Lacey's quick nod, Quinn stepped to her side and opened the passenger door to his SUV. Without a word, Lacey climbed in.

LACEY LOOKED across the table at Quinn. Susitna Burgers & Brew was one of the places they'd frequented over the years. In the days since she'd first met Quinn and then they crossed paths in Anchorage whenever they picked up trips together, they often ate here with other friends. Over the last few years, she'd spent less time in the area since she started her own business and Quinn had been away. She traced the edge of her wineglass, enjoying the comfort of being here. Flitting along the edges of her mind was the conversation with the doctor at the hospital. With a mental shake, she focused on Quinn. Her inconvenient attraction to him was suddenly just the distraction she needed. The light caught on his amber hair. His mouth, always in a half-smile, lifted a tad higher. "What?"

She shrugged. "It's nice to be here. I was trying to remember the last time I ate here. Pretty sure it was with you the summer before you left for your residency back East. We had just finished that trip to the refuge. Remember that couple who wanted to get back to the land?" At his nod, she continued. "After all that, I ran into them in Anchorage the following year and they were moving back to Los Angeles. They said they realized they could have a smaller ecological footprint in an urban area."

Quinn threw his head back with a laugh. "Seriously? I thought they were going to write a book and everything. So much for that, huh?"

"Guess so," she said with a laugh. She felt caught in Quinn's warm cognac gaze, heat rippling through her.

The waiter arrived and quickly cleared their table, leaving the check behind. Within moments, they were walking outside. A chilly autumn breeze gusted across the parking lot. Quinn drove toward the hotel where they had booked a shared suite months ago, long before Lacey had any inkling of her simmering attraction to Quinn. Were it not for the fact she was desperate to forget what the doctor had shared with her today and the churning anxiety she felt every time she thought about it, she'd be planning to run into the hotel and escape to her half of the shared suite. She didn't want to be alone with her thoughts though.

When they walked into the suite, Lacey tossed her backpack onto the floor in her room. "I'm gonna wash the trip off of me. Wanna watch a movie after?" she asked, nodding toward the television mounted on the wall in the sitting area between their rooms.

Quinn flashed a grin. "Sure thing."

Lacey walked out of her room a bit later, feeling clean and refreshed. Her body was practically humming in anticipation. As she'd slid the soap over her skin, she couldn't help but imagine how it would feel to have Quinn's hands on her. Quinn was standing beside the couch, flipping through the channels. His amber hair was damp. He wore a pair of sweatpants, which hung low on his hips, and a plain white t-shirt. Every inch of his muscled chest and abs were visible under the fitted cotton. She swallowed and aimed for nonchalant.

"Anything good on?" she asked, as she tugged the fluffy terry-cloth robe around her.

"Couple of sci-fi movies."

She plunked down on the couch and tucked her feet under her. "I like anything sci-fi, even the totally cheesy stuff."

Quinn joined her, sitting in the opposite corner of the couch. "Cheesy sci-fi it is then." He clicked a channel and leaned back into the cushions with a sigh.

For several minutes, Lacey tried to watch the movie, which was about some bizarre sea creature that somehow made its way into a lake and was terrorizing the town nearby. With only maybe a foot separating her and Quinn, she began calculating how to inch closer to him.

Have you lost your mind? Her rational brain asked, incredulous. *Maybe, maybe not. Quinn is totally hot and what would it hurt to have a little fun? Um, he's your friend and you maybe don't want to mess that up.* The second she thought that, an image of how vulnerable and strange she felt when she'd collapsed the other day flashed through her mind. She did *not* want to think about that. Restless and reckless, anxious to push any thoughts about her possible medical issues as far away as possible, she turned to Quinn and boldly closed the distance between them.

She rose up on her folded knees and swiveled to face him. His eyes widened as he turned his head to the side. She grinned, that reckless side of her devilishly pleased to find his lips mere inches from hers. She didn't wait to see what would happen and just acted. She leaned forward and brought her lips to his just as she slipped a hand around his neck. For a split second, he was completely still and then his lips gave under hers. Her wild gamble paid off when she traced her tongue along his lips and his palm stroked up her back, threading his fingers into her hair. He took over their kiss, his tongue stroking against hers and delving into her mouth. She most certainly forgot anything and everything as their kiss spiraled into a slow, hot, wet tease.

Quinn kissed thoroughly and completely—his tongue stroked in and out, he traced her lips, dropped a soft kiss on the corner of her mouth, and generally drove her wild with need. He angled her head to the side and sent a blazing trail of kisses down along the column of her throat. Frantic to get closer, she scrambled onto his lap, straddling him. She wore nothing under the robe save a pair of panties. A throaty sigh fell from her lips when she felt the hard, hot length of him against her. She couldn't hold back from rolling her hips, savoring the sharp spike of pleasure.

Suddenly Quinn lifted his head, going completely still. With her body nearly vibrating with longing and liquid need throbbing inside, she dragged her eyes open to find his waiting. His gaze was somber and almost pained. He was quiet for several beats, the only sound their mingled ragged breathing.

"Lace, what's this about?" he finally asked, his husky question tightening the need pulsing within her.

His question made her uncomfortable. She didn't want to answer and that reckless feeling nudged her again. She shook her head sharply and leaned forward to kiss him again. He shook his head. "Not until we talk."

Embarrassment rose within, colliding with the heat of desire and making her feel hot and flushed. She didn't know what he saw in her expression, but his eyes softened, which only served to further muddle her already confused feelings.

"Lace, don't get me wrong. You are one of the most amazing women I know and you're flat gorgeous. I'd be more than happy to let this keep going, but you're also a good friend. I don't want to mess up our friendship and until the last few weeks, I never thought you were even the least bit interested in me. Just tell me what you want and where this came from."

She took a deep breath and tried to marshal her thoughts. How could she tell him she was scared out of her mind and just wanted to lose herself in him? Underneath that thought rose the disconcerting truth that her attraction to him was a tiny bit frightening for her. Because he was her friend and if anyone had asked if she thought he'd be a good catch, she'd have resoundingly said yes. Which made her attraction to him all the more confusing. She'd always had this idea she'd do her life on her own. As life had gone along, she'd noticed most men steered clear of her. She'd chalked it up to men being intimidated by the fact she mostly did guy stuff. Here and there, she'd had a few casual flings, but sex had never been all that much fun, so she hadn't found it worthwhile to make much room for more in her life. This, this whatever the hell she felt right now with Quinn, was so far beyond anything she'd experienced, it both drew her close and frightened her. She wasn't accustomed to this pulsing physical need, nor to kisses that drove her beyond sanity.

Quinn's hand was still laced in her hair, and he started to slowly stroke his thumb along her nape, the subtle touch sending hot ripples through her. Emotion welled inside when she met his eyes again. She took a breath and let it out. She finally shrugged. "I don't know. I just, well, I wanted to kiss you so I did. Is that a problem? I mean, it seems like you might want something too." She shifted her hips for emphasis, a slight miscalculation because the subtle motion sent a sharp streak of pleasure scoring through her. Her channel, slick with need, throbbed.

Quinn took in a gulp of air and bit his lip, his breath coming out in a hiss. "Obviously, I want you. But there's no way in hell I'm having a one off night with you. I'm also a little worried about you. This isn't like you, so after what Dr. Clark told you today..."

She cut him off. "Don't even go there! This has nothing to do with that," she said, shaking her head sharply, angry he was so damn perceptive. She started to wiggle off his lap, but he gripped her hip with one strong hand.

"Okay, okay," he said, his voice low. "Then tell me where you're coming from."

She tried, oh she tried, to tamp down the emotion welling inside, but she couldn't. When she met his concerned gaze, a tear rolled down her cheek and then another and another. She shook her head again, as if she could will away her feelings, the anxious worry she might have an actual medical condition, the threat to the one thing she'd always been able to count on—her health and strength. Giving up when the tears just wouldn't quit, she dropped her head to his shoulder and let go.

His arms went around her and he let her cry. His palm stroked in slow passes up and down her back. He was quiet, seeming to know she didn't want platitudes. She just wanted to be comforted.

CHAPTER 3

Quinn opened one eye to find the room pitch black. He opened the other and read the time on the digital clock by the bed. It was just past two in the morning, and Lacey was curled up against his side. He'd sat with her while she cried for a few minutes, only to have her fall asleep in his arms. He'd gathered her up and carried her to her bed, intending to tuck her in and let her sleep. When he'd started to step away, she'd said his name, her voice raspy.

It was impossible for him not to curl up beside her when she said she didn't want to be alone. Problem was, now he was in the same situation as the other night in the tent—hard as a rock and not a damn thing to do about it. He realized he probably could do something about it based on Lacey's actions last night. Yet, that wasn't what he wanted. The first time he'd met Lacey, she'd blown him away—she was smart, strong, beautiful and a tomboy for the ages. She'd treated him like nothing more than a friend and never given him the slightest indication she was interested in anything else. So, he'd hewed to that role. When he'd met her at the airport a week before this latest trip, she'd looked at him differently. Desire flickered in the depths of her jade green eyes.

His conundrum now was what the hell to do. Because he didn't want to blow up their friendship, but he didn't want to just have a fling either. Lacey shifted restlessly in her sleep, her leg sliding against his. Her palm was warm against his chest. He lay there in the dark, wrestling between his body and mind. Fortunately, Lacey being sound asleep saved him from his body having its way because he wasn't quite ready to roll the dice on their friendship.

Early that afternoon, Quinn watched while the small plane carrying Lacey lifted into the air. She was on her way home, and he was on his way for a quick visit with his sister. Lacey had seemed surprised when he'd told her he might see her in Diamond Creek soon. One of the two medical offices there was hiring for a doctor since the doctor who'd established it was retiring. Quinn had made initial contact with them before the trip with Lacey and they'd just confirmed they wanted to schedule an interview with him. He'd always loved Diamond Creek, so it had been a no-brainer to consider moving there. Yet, what it might mean for possibilities with Lacey hadn't crossed his mind until last night.

He started his car and headed for his sister's home. He pulled up at her cute cabin roughly an hour later. She lived north of Anchorage in Willow Brook where they'd grown up. Her cabin was in a wooded area with other homes nearby, although not within sight. He strode up the steps of the A-frame cabin onto the front porch.

Amelia swung the door open to meet him. "Hey Quinn!" She flung her arms around him for a quick hug. When she stepped back, her smile was wide.

"Hey sis, how's it going?"

"Good, good. Come on in," she said, turning to walk back inside.

Quinn glanced around as he entered. The A-frame had a shared living room and kitchen in most of the downstairs with a bathroom and laundry area to the back. An open loft upstairs led to the bedroom. Amelia had built this home for herself while she was in college. At twenty-eight years old, she was six years younger than him and ran at life full force. She ran a small building and landscaping business. Even in Alaska where people were more accustomed to women not following along with typical gender roles, Amelia stood out. She was a damn good builder and could hold her own in just about any situation. Like Lacey, she also loved the outdoors and spent hours hiking, biking, camping and then some.

Amelia walked straight to the couch and plunked down on it, gesturing for Quinn to take a seat. "So how was your trip?" She twisted a lock of her honey-brown hair around her finger and looked over at him expectantly as he sat down in a rocking chair adjacent to the couch.

"It was great. Nice to get some time out there. Lacey and I escorted some photographers around Katmai. That's beautiful country in the fall."

Amelia grinned. "That's one of my favorite places, although last time I went there were a few too many bears for my comfort. How's Lacey? I haven't seen her in years it seems like."

"She's good, although she had some odd episodes while we were out. I pretty much forced her to get checked out at the hospital when we got back after she collapsed while we were walking to the plane. The doctor ran a few tests and thinks she might be on the way to an MS diagnosis. Lacey didn't want to talk about it, but she's pretty upset."

Amelia's cognac eyes widened. "Oh no. Is she okay?"

Quinn shrugged. "Yes and no. She's fine. This might be an isolated incident and it might not be. Even if she develops MS, she'll be fine. People live healthy for years with MS. Knowing Lacey though, she's not going to be too happy about it."

"Well, most people wouldn't be happy. If it comes to that, she'll just need some time to adjust. Did you agree with the doctor?" Amelia asked.

"MS was high on my list of suspicions based on her symptoms when she collapsed. But it could've been a bunch of other things. Honestly, she'll need to wait and see if she has any other symptoms." The worry he couldn't seem to push away flared inside again. He didn't like knowing how Lacey must be feeling with the uncertainty, not to mention his own concern for her.

Amelia was quiet for a moment. "Well, I hope she's okay. Next time you see her, tell her I said hey."

"You got it. Speaking of that, I'm waiting for a call back about an interview at that medical office down there."

Amelia grinned and gave a thumbs up. "Awesome! I told you you'd find a job in no time. Being a homegrown Alaskan with a fancy medical degree from Harvard, you can take your pick. No one's going to worry you can't hack life up here, and you've got the brains to do a damn good job. If I were going to move anywhere else in Alaska, Diamond Creek would be at the top of my list. Do you know when you're headed down there for the interview?"

"Not yet. They left a message they wanted to schedule, but we're in a game of phone tag. Hopefully soon because I'd rather not try to scrounge up a rental around here if I don't need it."

Quinn jumped topics. "So how's Mom?"

Amelia's gaze softened. "She's fine, Quinn. The place you

found in Palmer for her is working out. I thought maybe we could go visit her together this afternoon. They told me she should be done with rehab in another month or so and then she can move home again."

In the month before Quinn moved back to Alaska, their mother had been involved in a bad car accident. She'd simply been in the wrong place at the wrong time when an out of control camper swung sideways and crammed her car between the camper and a utility pole. She'd broken her hip and shattered her femur, along with breaking her other ankle, essentially immobilizing her. Amelia had come by her run at life attitude from their mother, so it was an understatement to say their mother was frustrated with the process of her recovery.

Their parents hadn't been together for many years. As such, their father lived out of state and barely stayed in touch. Making arrangements for their mother's medical care after she was stable enough to be moved out of ICU fell to Quinn and Amelia. She needed extensive rehabilitation to get her mobility back, so Quinn had walked off the plane in Alaska and rounded up some options for her as fast as he could. She'd refused to let him cancel his scheduled trip to Katmai, so he'd flown out the day after she was discharged from the hospital and into the rehabilitation center in Palmer. His mother was stubborn enough, he'd known she would be more annoyed with him if he cancelled his Katmai trip than if he hadn't. She expected her children to go at life just the way she did.

Relief washed through him. Knowing his mother, Quinn hadn't been too worried, but he knew it was probably driving her insane to be waiting through her rehabilitation. "Good to hear. When I did the tour there, it seemed like a good fit for her. They had a lot of younger patients, and I knew she'd get cranky otherwise."

Amelia threw her head back with a laugh. "Cranky's putting it nicely." Her laugh faded. "Honestly, I think this has been good for her. She was so happy to be out of the actual hospital that she's been enjoying her time at the rehab center. I know she likes to think she'll be strong as an ox forever, but she won't. I'm not happy she was in the car accident, but I'm glad to see how she's handled it."

Quinn leaned back, rocking slowly in the rocking chair. "Well, good then. When do you want to head over to see her?"

Amelia turned to look at the clock on the wall above her kitchen counter. "Whenever you want. I just need to be back here by five."

Hours later, Quinn walked to the doorway of the rehab center with his mother at his side, moving purposefully and probably too quickly with her walker. Amelia had left a little earlier to go to a planning meeting for a house she was working on. They reached the doors and he turned to face her. Sarah Haynes rolled her walker to a stop and flinched just barely. Quinn eyed her. "Don't push too hard, Mom. I heard your physical therapist tell you to make sure you don't put too much weight on that ankle too soon."

Sarah opened her mouth to reply and snapped it shut before shaking her head with a laugh. "She reminds me every day. I try to listen, but sometimes I forget."

"You look great. I can't believe how much progress you've made since I left a few weeks ago."

Sarah smiled, a devilish glint in her dark brown eyes. "I bet you didn't think I could follow doctor's orders."

Quinn chuckled. "I had my doubts. I figured the one thing that would keep you on track was knowing you might get out sooner if you did what they said."

Sarah lifted a hand and brushed her graying dark hair out of her eyes. Quinn and Amelia had gotten their amber hair and eyes from their father, although he'd been so distant in their lives, Quinn credited his mother with every-thing else, including the luck to be bright enough to stand out academically and the grit to love the wilderness the way he and Amelia did. Sarah lifted a shoulder in a small shrug. "That's exactly what kept me on track. The doctor said he might clear me to drive in a few weeks. He wants to see more mobility in my ankle first. Walking's the easy part. When they put me through the ankle circular rotations, it hurts like hell." His mother paused, her eyes assessing. "Amelia mentioned you were considering that medical clinic in Diamond Creek. I think you should go," she said firmly.

"Mom, I haven't even met with them yet. If it works out, I'll definitely go, but why does it matter to you?"

She pursed her lips and looked over at him thoughtfully. "Because you like the mountains and the ocean. Up here, all we have is the mountains. I'd rather have you nearby, but where you get the best of both worlds. Otherwise, you'll go gallivanting around the world again, and I'll miss you." Her eyes teared up as she spoke, and she swiped at them quickly.

Quinn stepped to the side of his mother's walker and hugged her. She wasn't one to show emotion often. She squeezed his hand tightly when he stepped away. "I always told you two to do whatever you wanted, but it doesn't mean I won't miss you. If you decide to go global again, you know I'll support you," she said with a firm nod.

"Mom, my stint overseas was great and I learned a lot, but I'm damn glad to be home. As soon as I know what's happening with the job in Diamond Creek, I'll let you know." He glanced at his watch. "Didn't Rose say she was meeting you at six?" he asked, referring to one of the women his mother had met at the rehab center. While his mother hadn't been thrilled to come here, she'd approached it the way she did everything—she accepted the reality and made it fun. In Quinn's brief visit, it was clear she'd endeared herself to the entire staff and befriended most everyone else staying there.

Sarah grinned. "She sure did. Well, then I'm off. Where are you staying tonight?"

"Hotel in Anchorage. I know I could stay at Amelia's, but she has zero privacy for company. I'm hoping to hear back from the clinic in Diamond Creek by tomorrow and maybe zip down there." He leaned over and dropped a kiss on his mother's cheek. "Go have dinner. I'll stop by again tomorrow."

At that, he gave a wave and headed to the parking lot. His phone buzzed when he climbed in his truck, indicating a text. He glanced at the screen. *Tell me it doesn't mean anything that I got that weird feeling in my legs again.*

Lacey's text sent his gut to churning. He knew she had a good chance of being okay even if she had MS, but it didn't change the fact he was worried about her. More worried than he would be for most because his guess was she would resist going to the doctor again. He considered for a moment before he replied. He elected to be blunt because tiptoeing around anything wasn't Lacey's style.

Can't tell you that bc I'd be lying. Take it easy tonight and go see your doctor tomorrow. No joke.

He started his car and flicked the heat on since the evening autumn air was as chilly as it could get without being below freezing. Her reply was swift.

I might have preferred you lie. Promise I'm taking it easy. I'll think about going to the doctor. When did you say you'd be here?

He grinned, sensing she was plenty annoyed, but not being stupid just yet. At the thought of seeing her again, a jolt of electricity rushed through him, making him forget his worry. He wasn't quite sure how to handle his long-buried attraction to Lacey coming to life like a brush fire after she'd kissed him. He mentally shook himself.

I'll hold you to that promise. Not sure when I'll be there. Depends on when I hear back. I'll let you know.

K. Resting right now.

He grinned again and slipped his phone back in his pocket. When he walked back into the hotel suite, his eyes landed on the couch and he remembered the feel of Lacey straddling him.

CHAPTER 4

"Hey! Give me that," Lacey demanded as she carefully tried to free the chunk of her hair held tightly in her niece's fist.

Holly giggled and yanked a little harder. At the sound of a muffled laugh, Lacey glanced over her shoulder to see her sister Marley laughing where she stood by the kitchen counter. "I'm sure she does this all day to you, so feel free to laugh," Lacey replied wryly as she gently wiggled her finger into Holly's hand. Holly slowly released her hair and clutched the collar of her jacket instead. At ten months old, Holly was a bundle of motion and curiosity. Lacey had spent most of her life convinced children weren't for her and then along came her absolutely adorable niece. Lacey reached above her head and slowly lifted Holly off of her shoulders to bring her to her lap. Holly grinned at her with her soft green eyes. "Mwah!" Lacey dropped a noisy kiss on her cheek and handed Holly a brightly colored fabric parrot, which Holly immediately stuffed in her mouth.

Lacey had stopped by for a visit with her older sister and some Holly time. She'd been out of sorts since her trip and was hoping her sister could help her settle inside. At thirty-two, Marley was two years older than her and the smartest person Lacey knew. Lacey couldn't have been happier when Marley moved back to Diamond Creek two years ago and fell head over heels in love with Gage Hamilton. Aside from being generally awesome because he loved Marley, Gage had also reopened Last Frontier Lodge, which endeared him even more to Lacey because she loved to ski and now she had free family passes to ski to her heart's content all winter long. Marley ran the website for the lodge, along with her own tech applications business. Growing up together, they'd always called themselves Brains and Brawn with Marley being the Brains and Lacey the Brawn.

Lacey was trying to work up to telling someone besides Quinn about her episodes, but she wasn't sure she was up for it yet. She liked being Brawn and thinking about falling on her face twice didn't exactly live up to the image. She glanced over her shoulder to Marley. "Need some help?"

Marley turned, holding up two mugs as she did. "Coffee on the way!" Marley walked across the room and set the mugs down on the coffee table. "I got a new one shot espresso maker while you were gone, and I still haven't quite mastered it. Tell me what you think."

Lacey leaned over, holding Holly in place with one hand, and curled her other hand around the mug. Once she was upright again, she took a slow sip. "Ooh! It's yummy. Maybe you don't think you've mastered it, but it's delicious."

Marley grinned. "Oh good! It seems to tolerate my fiddling, but half the time I don't know what I'm doing. Delia insisted I needed something other than the drip coffee maker we had, but this thing has dials and adjustments, and I have no idea what to do with all of them."

Lacey shook her head and grinned. "Delia likes the best of everything. I gotta say, this is definitely better than what your old coffee maker produced."

Marley sat down on the couch and crossed her legs. "Enough about the coffee, how was Katmai?"

Lacey instantly felt hot and rattled inside. Katmai brought two things to mind: Quinn and her churning, burning attraction to him, and the disquieting episodes she'd experienced. Holly wiggled on Lacey's lap, distracting her. Lacey eased her onto the couch where Holly promptly crawled over to her mother, dragging her parrot with her. Lacey laughed softly as Holly wiggled up against Marley' leg.

Lacey aimed to keep her response casual. "The trip was great. We couldn't have asked for better weather—cool and dry during the day. On the chilly side at night, but it wasn't anything worse than what I expected."

"How's Quinn? This is the first year he's been back since he was away, right?"

"He's great. He landed back in Alaska only a few weeks before we left for Katmai. You might see him soon actually. He's expecting to hear back about an interview with the medical clinic here."

"Oh that would be great! With Dr. Daniels retiring, rumor for a while was they might close Coastal Medical Clinic, but then I heard he decided to try to find someone to replace him. Quinn would be perfect. Do you know when that might happen?"

"He told me he was waiting for another call to schedule a meeting. I'm guessing sometime soon."

Marley turned her head, purposefully swinging her auburn ponytail out of Holly's reach. "I keep thinking I should chop my hair off, but I can't quite bring myself to do it. I figure she has to grow out of this hair grabbing thing someday, right?" Marley asked with a laugh.

Lacey shrugged. "Maybe so. Your ponytail trick seems to work." She glanced over at Marley's hair, held high in a ponytail atop her head. She and Marley shared the same coloring, although her hair was slightly darker than Marley's. Otherwise, they had the same green eyes and lightly freckled skin.

Marley's cell phone buzzed, and she fumbled it out of her pocket while playing a gentle tug of war with Holly and her parrot. She glanced at the screen. "Have to grab this. It's the guy from the internet company who's upgrading our wireless."

Lacey nodded and took another swallow of coffee while she looked out over the view. Marley and Gage lived at the ski lodge in a private apartment above the restaurant. They had a view for the ages with the mountains rising behind the lodge and Kachemak Bay glinting under the sun in the corner. The ski slopes were void of snow for now, although that could change any day now. It was mid-October and winter was chasing on the heels of autumn. A few hikers were visible along the trails in the trees between the ski slopes. Gage had opened up the lodge property year-round to hikers, bikers and more, so when the snow wasn't flying, there were plenty of other ways for locals and tourists to enjoy the area.

Lacey scanned the view, reflexively looking toward her parents' property nearby. The small cabin where she was staying was visible through the spruce forest, its bright red roof making it easy to find. She and Marley had grown up beside Last Frontier Lodge and skied here when they were little. She mentally flinched when the recollections of her collapse to the ground and again in Quinn's arms flashed through her mind. She did *not* want to have to worry about her health. She thrived on being strong and living on the edge. It just wouldn't work for her to have to be anything else. She was determined those episodes would be just that —a few odd episodes that would never repeat themselves.

After Marley finished her call, she glanced over to Lacey. "Are you okay?" Marley asked.

Lacey snapped back to the moment, kicking her worries about what the doctor said to the curb. "Where'd that question come from?" she asked, feeling snippy Marley might have noticed something amiss.

In the few minutes Marley had been on the phone, Holly had instantly fallen asleep and was slumped against Marley's leg, her stuffed parrot finally free from her clutching hand. Marley carefully lifted Holly and set her inside a cushioned seat between them on the couch. Holly promptly settled in, never even opening her eyes.

Marley reached for her mug of coffee and eyed Lacey. "Because you just look, I don't know, like something's bothering you. Really bothering you."

Lacey shrugged and did her damnedest to keep her expression neutral, annoyed as she was at her sister's perceptiveness. "Nah. I'm fine. Just a little tired. Those trips are a blast, but it usually takes me a few days to get my groove back."

Marley took a sip of coffee and nodded slowly. She didn't look convinced, but she let the topic drop. "Any more trips for you before the snow flies?"

"Nope. I promised myself I'd stop the winter trips and I'm holding to it. It's too damn cold. I've got some booked through the company, but I won't be the guide. A few of the guys Quinn and I used to work with are leading all three I've booked so far. They seem to like freezing their tails off, so I'll do the bookings and handle all the prep, but the rest is up to them."

Marley laughed softly. "I wondered if you'd be able to stick to that. Mom and Dad'll be thrilled. They did their best not to worry, but I know they didn't love it when you were out in the middle of nowhere in the winter."

"I know they worried. I get my fill of winter skiing right here, and that's enough these days." Lacey's mind spun to how much their parents would worry if they knew she'd collapsed twice during her last trip and Quinn had dragged her to the hospital when they landed in Anchorage. She hated when people fussed over her. Those episodes were over and she'd be fine.

* * *

QUINN CRESTED the hill and guided his truck into the viewing area beside the highway. Diamond Creek lay at the bottom of this hill, spread out against the backdrop of Kachemak Bay. Many a postcard of this exact view had been mailed from Diamond Creek all over the world simply because it captured the spectacular beauty of the area. Diamond Creek was renowned for its beauty due to its stunning location on sparkling Kachemak Bay with the mountains rising up behind it and circling the bay on all sides. Glaciers winked under the sun where they slipped between mountain peaks and dipped into the ocean. Quinn had always loved this part of Alaska. The weather was a tad less harsh in the Southcentral area, and it contained the best of both worlds with the mountains and the ocean beside each other. When he was growing up, his mother used to bring him and Amelia down for long weekends here.

It was quite true that he was interested in the job here because he loved the area, but ever since his mind-blowing kiss with Lacey, he was wondering what else Diamond Creek might hold for him. He leaned against the railing and looked out over the water. Yellowed birch leaves blew loose in front of him. Autumn was blowing away with the brisk wind, a bite of winter held within. He scanned the view, savoring the sense of being back in Alaska in a place he loved. In all his travels, he never captured the feeling of being in Alaska—on the edge of the wild with the comfort of being home. He turned away from the view and climbed back in his car. He'd texted Lacey yesterday to let her know he'd be here today. He'd planned to stay in one of the local hotels downtown, but Lacey insisted he stay at Last Frontier Lodge, courtesy of her sister. In days gone by, he'd have thought nothing of it, but between his lingering concern over her health scare and his muddled feelings over his long-dormant desire for her coming to life like a flash fire, he wasn't sure how to interpret anything with her.

He figured he'd raise more questions if he demurred and didn't stay at the lodge, so he followed the winding road up the mountainside once he reached Diamond Creek. Within a few minutes of arriving at the lodge, Lacey's sister met him at the reception desk. Marley looked remarkably like Lacey with a softer edge to her, but the same auburn hair, green eyes and fit and curvy figure. Quinn didn't feel the slightest twinge of attraction to her. Only Lacey had that effect on him.

"Quinn! It's good to see you," Marley said, pulling him into a quick hug.

"The same for you," Quinn said as he stepped back. "Thanks for offering to let me stay here."

"Of course! You're welcome anytime. You've been overseas since we reopened, so it'll be a good chance for you to see the place. You like skiing as much as Lacey, so once the snow flies, I'm betting you'll be here plenty," Marley said with a grin just as a tall man came through the door behind the reception desk and stepped around it to Marley's side.

Quinn figured this must be Marley's husband and the man responsible for resurrecting Last Frontier Lodge. He knew from Lacey that Gage was a former Navy SEAL and he certainly looked the part. He was in prime physical condition and carried himself with a quiet alertness. His dark hair and gray eyes only emphasized the sense of power and perception emanating from him. He slipped an arm around Marley's shoulders and nodded in Quinn's direction.

"Gage Hamilton," he offered, holding his hand out for a shake.

Quinn shook his hand and returned the nod. "Quinn Haynes. I was just thanking Marley for letting me stay here, so let me thank you as well. I told Lacey this wasn't necessary, but she insisted. I haven't had a chance to look around, but I can tell you've done an amazing job getting this place back up to speed. Last time I was here, the whole place was boarded up and looked a little worse for wear."

Gage flashed a grin. "Thanks. I couldn't have pulled it off without Marley's help and Don and Delia. Marley took care of everything I didn't know how to handle, and Don and Delia made sure I didn't mess up too much."

Marley flushed and shook her head. "You never give yourself enough credit." She caught Quinn's eyes. "Does Lacey know you're here yet?"

"She knew I was coming today, but I came here first. She said she's next door."

Marley nodded. "She's staying at a little cabin on our parents' property. It's right through the trees," she said, gesturing generally in the air.

Gage stepped away. "Need help carrying anything in?"

Quinn lifted the strap to his backpack. "I've got everything in here."

"Let me show you your room. Follow me," Marley said, quickly turning to stride toward a staircase that curved along the wall in the circular reception area.

"Nice to meet you," Quinn said, catching Gage's eyes.

"Same. I'll see you in a bit. We're meeting for dinner later."

At that, Quinn turned and followed Marley upstairs. She led him down a long hallway to a corner suite. The room offered a stunning view of the mountains behind the lodge with a sliver of Kachemak Bay visible to the far side of the mountains. Quinn looked to Marley. "This is gorgeous, but it's much more than I need," he said, taking in the luxurious suite with its king bed, small seating area and kitchenette. "I hope you're not giving up bookings for me."

Marley put her hands on her hips. "Don't be ridiculous. You're a family friend, so you get to stay. We always keep one empty suite for friends and family, so don't even worry about it."

Quinn chuckled and let his backpack slide off his shoulder. "So we're having dinner later?"

"We are. It's not set in stone, but we often meet with friends in the restaurant. Lacey made us promise we'd get together tonight, so you'd better be prepared for some socializing." Marley paused and looked out over the view before turning back to him. Her expression sobered. She looked at him for a long moment, as if considering what she meant to say. "Did something happen on the trip to Katmai?" she finally asked.

Quinn was startled and quickly schooled his expression to neutral. He'd have thought Lacey would have told her family about what happened and her subsequent visit to the hospital. As he stood there, his mind whirring through ways to respond to Marley's question, he realized he shouldn't be surprised. Lacey wouldn't like talking about any problems with her health. He knew perfectly well that even if Lacey's symptoms progressed and a formal MS diagnosis was made, she'd still be able to live the life she wanted, albeit with a few accommodations for treatment and planning if she was in an active period of symptoms. MS was a disease of waxing and waning. Many people went years without a relapse of symptoms. Lacey might never have another episode, although her text about the 'weird feeling in her legs' didn't indicate that. He mentally shook himself. He didn't need to play doctor right now. It would piss Lacey off if he did. He needed to answer Marley's question and figure out how the hell to do so while protecting Lacey's privacy.

"Uh, why do you ask?" he finally countered.

Marley crossed her arms and all but glared at him. "Okay, what happened?"

Quinn mentally sighed. "How about you tell me what you're worried about? We had a fairly uneventful back-country trip, all things considered." His words were factually true, given that Lacey's two episodes had been minor and the only thing out of the ordinary that happened. He didn't know how to navigate this with Marley because he knew she and Lacey were close, and Marley was clearly just as perceptive as her sister.

Marley let her arms fall and sighed. "I don't know. It's only been a few days since she's been home, but she just seems a little off. Something's bothering her, but when I ask, she gets all prickly. Other than that, it's just a gut feeling, a sister thing."

Quinn leaned an elbow against the counter beside them and ran a hand through his hair. "Look, how about you ask Lacey instead of me?"

"Because she won't tell me anything!" Marley threw her hands up in exasperation.

"Do me a favor and don't put me in the middle. I promise you if I were seriously concerned about Lacey, I'd let you know. Trust your gut and make her talk to you. That's all I can say."

Marley's eyes softened. "Okay, okay. I get it. You don't want her to get pissed at you. Well then, I guess I'll have to make her tell me. She's usually the bossy one, but I can be bossy too," she said with a wry grin.

She glanced to the clock above the windows. "Meet us in the restaurant downstairs at five-thirty. Otherwise, make yourself at home and wander around."

She gave a small wave and exited the room. When the door clicked shut, Quinn took a deep breath and let it out with a groan. He'd just half-lied to Marley and he didn't like it one bit. The truth was he was seriously concerned about Lacey, but not because he was overly concerned about her health. He was concerned about how she was handling what happened. It really could be nothing and never happen again, but it wasn't boding well for Lacey to hide her check up at the hospital from Marley. In all the time he'd known her, Lacey and Marley had been close. For her to hide something meant it was bothering the hell out of her.

He pushed away from the counter and slipped his phone out of his pocket. Instead of wondering how Lacey was doing, he'd go see her.

CHAPTER 5

*L*acey walked down the stairs in the cabin and paused at the bottom to look out the windows. The small cabin where she was temporarily staying was on her parents' property. Years ago, her parents used to rent it out during summers for extra money, but they'd stopped doing that for a while. The rental where she'd been staying changed owners, so she'd moved here while she figured out where she'd stay next. The cabin was cozy and cute. The upstairs was a loft with a bedroom and bathroom, while the downstairs was one large open space that contained the kitchen and living room with a small bathroom and laundry at the back. The entire wall facing the mountains and Kachemak Bay was windows, which came to a point at the roof in the center. Fluffy clouds drifted across the view. The snow had fallen a little lower on the mountains across the bay, heralding winter's coming arrival at the lower elevations. Wind scudded across the bay, ruffling the surface.

Lacey turned away and glanced around the room, her eyes landing on the cheery red woodstove anchoring the living room. She was actually looking forward to winter in the cabin. Winters were warm and inviting with the wood-stove and the view of the snow-covered landscape. Both she and Marley had taken their turns with temporary stays here. It was lovely and held many childhood memories because when it wasn't rented out, she and Marley used to have camp-outs here for fun.

She stepped off the bottom of the stairs and strode to the kitchen counter. She'd gone for an afternoon run on the beach and pushed herself hard. It was chilly enough outside that she'd gotten cold. After a steaming shower, she still wanted something else to warm her and another cup of coffee would do the trick. As she waited for the coffee maker to beep, her phone buzzed. Snagging it off the counter, she saw a text from Quinn.

I'm at the lodge. Tell me how to find you.

Go on the back deck and look up the closest slope. You'll see a trail through the trees on the right. Follow it.

A flutter on anticipation swirled in her belly and a smile curled her lips. In any case, she'd have been happy to have Quinn visit. He was a good friend and easy to be around. Now, it was something else altogether. She must have replayed their kiss the other night a few hundred times already. Though a huge part of her was still all a muddle over this new attraction to him, she couldn't seem to stop it. It also gave her something else to obsess about other than what might or might not be happening with her health. In the days since she'd been home, she'd had two more times when her legs felt funny and weak. Both times, she'd conveniently been home alone, so she'd sat down on the couch and waited until the feeling passed. The second her mind started to ponder that, she shied away, her thoughts landing on Quinn.

A loud beep interrupted her reverie about the fact she'd learned Quinn was one hell of a kisser. With a shake of her head, she got her coffee ready. Just as she was taking a sip, she saw Quinn stepping out through the trees on the side of the field behind the cabin. She went out on the back deck to meet him. His grin flashed when he saw her, and he closed the remaining distance at a jog. A gust of wind blew her damp hair wild as he reached the deck. Her gaze soaked him in—his amber hair and eyes, his warm grin, and his body of nothing but muscle. Now that she knew what his body felt like, her mind flipped to the feel of his sculpted chest and his hot, hard… Screech. *Oh. My. God. Stop it. You can't just drool over him all the time. That's so not you. Act normal.*

She looked up at him and saw his eyes darken, immediately sending a jolt of heat through her. Butterflies amassed in her belly and her pulse lunged forward. Quinn moved smoothly as he stepped to her and enveloped her in a hug. When he stepped back, she experienced a flash of longing so intense, it startled her. She curled both hands around her coffee cup as if it could somehow anchor her and keep her from climbing all over him.

"Hey," he said simply.

"Hey yourself. Are you all settled over at the lodge?"

"Of course. Marley showed me my room. Got to meet Gage too. Gotta say, I bet you love having that place right here. You can ski through the trees if you want." He paused and turned slowly in a circle, scanning the view. From her cabin, part of the lodge was visible in the distance, but otherwise the cabin was protected from view of any other homes and nestled into a cluster of spruce with a small field behind it and nothing but mountains and the bay beyond that. When his gaze came back to her, he arched a brow. "Can't beat the view or the privacy here."

She grinned. "I know. Not too shabby, although it's hard to find anywhere around here that doesn't have a great view. Come on in."

Once they were inside, she got him some coffee and plunked down on the couch, gesturing for him to join her.

Usually, she'd have no trouble easing into chatter about whatever was going on, but she was too wired right now and uncertain what to say about anything. There was the elephant in the room of what seemed to be the mutual attraction between them, and then there was the fact Quinn happened to be the only person close to her who knew anything about her possible medical concerns. Independently, each of those issues would have made her feel out of sorts and uncomfortable with him. Lump them together and she was practically tongue-tied.

If he noticed anything amiss, he ignored it. He took a swallow of coffee and grinned. "Almost as good as mine."

"Hey! I can make good coffee too," she protested, batting at him with her free hand.

He chuckled and shrugged. "I suppose." He took another swallow and leaned back, entirely comfortable and relaxed even though his rangy form barely fit on the small couch. "So, I hear we're having dinner with some people tonight?"

"We sure are. Marley mentioned she hadn't seen you since you went away to finish up medical school, so I rounded up anyone I thought you might know. Ever since the lodge got up and running, we get together there a lot, so it's not really a thing. You might meet a few new people. Gage's brother and sister have both moved up here..." She paused to consider who else she'd invited. "You've met Delia before, right?"

"Oh yeah. You and Marley grew up with her, right? Think I met her one of the other times I came through here."

"Probably. Anyway, it'll be fun. So what's the update with your interview?"

"I meet with them tomorrow. They've already reviewed everything. It sounds promising, but Dr. Daniels has made it clear his decision will be personal. Sounds like he wants to make sure whoever takes over the practice is a good fit for the patients and the community."

"Dr. Daniels grew up in Diamond Creek, so he won't let someone into that clinic unless he feels good about it. I ran into him the other day though, and he asked me about you. Seeing as Diamond Creek's pretty small when it comes to locals, he knew we worked together. Of course I told him you'd be perfect for what he's looking for. Even though we're friends, I wouldn't have said so if I didn't mean it. Maybe you didn't grow up in Diamond Creek, but you're an Alaskan through and through, and you love this area. That, plus the fact you're a genius."

Quinn threw his head back with a laugh. "Wow, I guess I should have put you down as an official reference."

Lacey flushed, suddenly self-conscious. She'd meant every word she'd said to Dr. Daniels about Quinn, but talking about it reminded her just what a great guy he was. She wasn't used to thinking about him in any category other than friend. "Anyway, he seems pretty hopeful. Did he tell you his eventual plan is to sell the practice to whoever he hires?"

Quinn nodded. "I didn't know it when I applied, but he mentioned it when we spoke the other day."

"How do you feel about that? I mean, it's kind of a commitment."

"Like I told you, I'm back in Alaska to stay. Diamond Creek's always been one of my favorite places to visit, so it works for me. I love to travel, but I want my home base here," he said firmly.

Lacey's stomach kept doing little flips every so often. Thinking about Quinn living right here in Diamond Creek sent it spinning with flutters rippling through her. She had never, *never*, thought about a long-term relationship with anyone. But the idea of something like that with Quinn, well that did strange things to her insides.

* * *

QUINN SET his empty coffee cup down and looked over at Lacey. She seemed wound tight with her heel lightly bouncing against the sofa and one hand twirling a lock of auburn hair. He couldn't say he wasn't wound tight, what with the gates opened on his desire for her. He'd spent most of his drive here lecturing himself on how important it was to not blow his friendship up with her. He almost laughed aloud right now. The moment he'd seen her across the field as he walked to her cabin, it was as if an electric current crackled to life in the air between them. He marveled he'd done such a damn good job of snuffing out his initial spark for her, he was now stumbling under the onslaught of longing. The slightest indication from Lacey she returned his interest and he was done for. Although the other night had been a bit more than slight.

Lacey had been staring out the window and turned to him, her jade gaze colliding with his. The worry reflected there almost physically pained him, and his mental meandering stopped abruptly as he focused on her. "Marley's worried about you," he said before he had a chance to think.

Lacey drained her coffee and set the mug on the table. "I know," she said with a soft sigh. "Did she ask you about me?"

"Yeah. Said she was worried and wanted to know if something happened on the trip." He paused to gauge Lacey's response. When she stayed quiet, her eyes watching and waiting, he continued. "How come you haven't told her about your falls and what the doctor said?" Tension coiled inside once he asked the question, worried about how she might respond. She surprised him.

"Because it scares me and I don't want to talk about it," she said bluntly.

The twirling speed of her hand picked up as that lock of

auburn hair slid in a circle around her index finger, again and again and again. Lacey was open in some ways, but guarded in others. She was the first to be warm and sensitive with a friend and the last to ever be vulnerable enough to let a friend offer the same in return.

Quinn decided he'd already ripped the scab off the topic, so he might as well keep going. "Lace, it's not like anyone would be excited about a possible MS diagnosis, or any potentially long-term medical issue. If it comes to that, there are plenty of treatment options. You should know that the most common form of MS is relapsing-remitting MS. Symptoms come and go and some people go years without any. Many don't experience any symptoms in between attacks. Normally, I wouldn't even want to speculate on whether you actually have MS, but I can tell you're doing a bang up job of obsessing about it. Instead of blowing it up in your mind, focus on facts. If, and that's still an if, you get diagnosed with MS, there's a good chance you'll be like most people and your symptoms will wax and wane. An MS diagnosis isn't a death sentence, not even close. Most people with MS live just as long as those without it."

He paused and waited. Her gaze was like a laser beam on him, intent and focused. "Long story short, it's not going to help at all for you to get all worked up over this. Some people go years before another episode like what you had in Katmai. No doctor will formally diagnose you until they can isolate more than one episode and two areas of nerve damage. If you have MS, it's already looking like it's relapsing-remitting. If you can, try to stop worrying. I know how close you and Marley are, so maybe you might want to talk to her."

Lacey blinked rapidly and turned to stare out the windows again. "Did you tell her anything?" she asked, her tone only slightly annoyed.

Under the circumstances, Quinn considered that amazing. "Nope. She asked if something happened and because I didn't want to piss you off, I didn't tell her. I told her to ask you. I figure you either tell her yourself, or she'll harass you until you do."

Lacey turned back to him and sighed, finally releasing the lock of hair. Her green eyes were bright, just bright enough Quinn suspected she was blinking back tears. His heart clenched, and he had to hold himself back from reaching over and hauling her into his arms. He could tell her all day long she didn't need to be so worried, but she had to figure it out on her own.

"I heard everything you just told me, and I took those materials Dr. Clark gave me. It's not like I think I'm going to die. It's just…ugh…" She chewed on her lip, staring at the floor. "My nickname when we were growing up was Brawn, okay? I love what I do. I love pushing myself to the limit physically. I've always been healthy and strong. Even with all the crazy stuff I do, I haven't gotten hurt. Now this. It's making me crazy! I mean, I was just standing there and I fell on my ass. Then, all I was doing was walking to meet the plane and it happened again. And why do you and Dr. Clark keep calling it a single episode? I didn't even mention that I felt weak the day before and had to stop and catch my balance on a tree! That's three times, not once." She threw her hands up and leaned her head back against the couch. When she rolled her head to the side, her eyes were still slightly damp, but she looked plenty annoyed.

Uncertain which of her comments to reply to, Quinn started with the simplest. "Dr. Clark referred to it as a single episode because usually the symptoms will last for a period of time and then fade away. I wish you'd mentioned you'd felt weak another time, but whatever." He paused and waited before jumping to the more difficult part of what she said. "As for you being Brawn…" A chuckle rolled out of him as he said her childhood nickname, which earned him a wide grin from Lacey. "…you'll still be just who you are. If, remember the 'if' part of this, you need to do a few things to manage your symptoms, you will. You've already backed off of your winter trips, so it's not like you can't shift gears. Instead of thinking worst case scenario, how about you try to wait and see?"

Lacey's grin faded as she looked at him. "I'll try, but I'm really good at getting all worked up over things."

"This from the woman who once skied off a cliff in front of me and landed like a champ."

Lacey grinned again and lifted one shoulder in a shrug. "That's different. This stuff," she pointed to her head "is all up here." She couldn't let herself start thinking she had MS. She was too strong for that. She knew, just knew, those weird episodes would become a distant memory.

"I know."

Lacey took a deep breath and sighed elaborately. "Of course you understand. You're a good friend, so you'll be nice and put up with my obsessing and wish I'd shut the hell up," she said with a roll of her eyes.

He shook his head. "I'm not wishing you'd shut up. I'm wishing for your own sake, you'd stop obsessing. Oh, and talk to Marley. Otherwise, she's going to keep bugging me and I can only hold her off for so long."

Lacey threw a small pillow at him and stood up quickly. "Fine. I'll talk to her. Wanna take the long trail back to the lodge on our way to dinner?"

CHAPTER 6

$\mathcal{L}$acey felt the heat of Quinn's thigh nearly searing her. They were seated in the corner booth at the lodge restaurant with enough friends and family that their gathering had spilled over to another table nearby. She'd managed the first hour or so of dinner just fine. Now, with a few glasses of wine in her and being crowded up against Quinn because Gage's sister Jessa was on the other side of her, well, it was safe to say she was practically on fire.

"Yoo hoo," Ginger Nash said, waving her hand back and forth from across the booth.

Lacey whipped her head up, catching the motion of Ginger's hand out of the corner of her eye. "Huh?"

Ginger's blue eyes narrowed, a hint of mischief held within her gaze. "I asked you two times in a row if you wanted to be in for Diamond Creek Batters next spring."

Lacey wasn't about to share she'd been zoning out over her replay of her kiss with Quinn the other night, so she nodded before she even considered her answer.

"Yes!" Ginger declared. "We've got a full team. Now I

have to find some back ups." Her eyes swung to Quinn. "How about you? You're moving here, right?"

Quinn chuckled and shrugged. "Maybe, but it's not definite. What's Diamond Creek Batters?"

"I'm sure Dr. Daniels will hire you, so you'll be here," Ginger replied firmly, her shiny dark hair swinging with her nod. "Diamond Creek Batters is one of our local league baseball teams. Every other year, I help manage it. We've won the league championship for four years straight now, so you'll be joining a winning team."

Ginger's satisfied grin elicited a laugh from her husband Cam. He looked to Quinn. "No need to bow to her pressure, but she won't let up either. I'm playing too, so if that sways your decision…" Cam's golden brown eyes canted down to Ginger, his love for her evident in his gaze.

"Okay, count me in. If I end up moving here for sure, I'll play. No promises I'm amazing, but I do all right," Quinn replied.

Lacey's heart gave a thump. The idea that Quinn could be part of her daily world sent a spin of longing through her. Between that and being surrounded by a few dear friends who'd been blessed enough to find love recently, it was hard not to wonder what it could be like. She felt rattled about the depth of her attraction to Quinn and these unfamiliar thoughts about relationships. For crying out loud, her sister had fallen head over heels with Gage and not once had it crossed Lacey's mind that she might want something like that. Not until now and not until her attraction to Quinn shot through her like lightning.

Conversation carried on around her with her body suffused with heat and hyperaware of every subtle motion of Quinn beside her. With the booth crowded, she was pressed up against his side, so it was impossible to avoid being close. Not that she wanted to avoid it, mind you, but it was pushing her to her limits.

"Lacey, didn't you say you were booking a few trips to the Arctic Wildlife Refuge next year?" Marley asked from the table nearby.

Lacey glanced over and nodded. "I already have two parties scheduled. For both trips, there's room left. Who wants to go?"

Garrett Hamilton, Gage's brother, raised his hand. "I want to take Nick out there. He can't stop talking about it, so I figure we should try it once. I don't know if the trips you do would be the best fit for an eight year old though. Whaddya think?"

Delia, Garrett's wife and manager of the lodge restaurant, shook her head slowly. "I don't know about this." Delia caught Lacey's eyes. "Am I crazy to let them even think about this?"

Lacey shook her head with a smile. "Not really. If they take the family trip I've coordinated, they'll be with two other families with kids, so the whole thing will be light hiking." She looked to Garrett. "Call me tomorrow and we'll discuss dates."

Garrett flashed a grin, his blue eyes twinkling. He and Delia were a pair of opposites. He was dark with a sharp edge to him, witty and brilliant with a heart of gold. Delia, with her honey gold hair and warm blue eyes, softened his edges, while he eased her tendency to worry. Lacey watched when Delia rolled her eyes at his glee and experienced another odd pang in her chest.

What is it with you tonight? Everything you see makes you think about Quinn. Oh, and how about you get a handle on what he's doing to your body? You'd think you'd never been turned on before. Her tendency toward internal sarcasm was at its worst when she felt uncertain because she hated feeling uncertain. And boy, oh boy, did this whole thing with Quinn make her feel like she was bumbling along. Truth was, she didn't have a ton of experience with men outside the realm of being the friend.

Time passed in a strange warp between the heat suffusing her and her difficulty focusing on conversation around her. The gathering slowly broke apart until only she and Quinn were left. Somewhere along the way, Quinn had gotten up from the booth and was leaning against the table nearby. Delia poked her head out through the swinging door that led into the kitchen. "Need anything else before I shut everything down back here?" she asked, her eyes flicking from Lacey to Quinn.

Lacey shook her head. "Nope. Just getting ready to walk home. Dinner was amazing, as always."

Delia threw a smile over her shoulder as she turned away, letting the door swing shut behind her. Lacey looked over at Quinn. A waiter was quietly circling the restaurant, clearing tables and flicking off lights. Quinn's face was shadowed in the low lights. When he caught her eyes, electricity arced across the space between them. Lacey's pulse rocketed ahead and the need beating like a drum within her all evening struck a higher note, one she couldn't ignore. She looked over at Quinn. Even when he was relaxed, he exuded quiet strength and power. One of his hands rested on the table, and her eyes traced the corded muscles of his arm. He wore a black t-shirt, which made his amber skin stand out in contrast. He was amber all over from his hair to his eyes to his skin—just golden and so damn tempting she could hardly bear it. He pushed away from the table and reached for his jacket hanging on a hook by the booth.

"I'll walk you back," he said, his low voice sending a prickle of heat through her.

She couldn't seem to speak, but she managed a nod and stood. They walked out onto the back deck. The cold air slammed into her. It was a balm to the heat within. She paused at the foot of the stairs and looked up beyond the mountains. The sky was clear, the stars bright against the backdrop. Only a sliver of the moon was visible, hanging low over the mountains. Their breath misted the air. Without a word, they began walking. She was acutely aware of his presence beside her as they walked across the ski slope toward the trail through the trees leading to her cabin. Their footsteps crunched on the frost-covered grass. Somewhere between the lodge and her cabin, she made a decision. Consequences be damned, she would have at least one night with Quinn. Beyond the constant beat of desire drumming within, she was desperate for the escape and had given up on talking herself out of how she felt. The draw was too strong. In the chilly autumn night, she could feel his presence like a magnet drawing her closer and closer.

When they reached her cabin, Quinn followed her up the stairs and to the door. When she opened it, she glanced back at him. He stood there quietly. He started to speak, but she cut him off when she grabbed his hand and yanked him inside behind her. She felt reckless and edgy inside, unable to contain the desire streaking through her in waves. She looked up, straight into his eyes. She scanned his face—his chiseled features, an old scar that slashed on the lower side of his jaw courtesy of the edge of a rock when he fell while scaling a steep peak once, his full lips, the only softness on his face other than his warm eyes. When she reached his eyes again, they were dark, the desire she felt reflected in their depths.

While a small voice inside cautioned her she might be crazy, Lacey didn't care just now. A gust of wind blew through the door. Quinn kicked it shut quickly. She'd thought to leave a light on when they left earlier. The light from the loft filtered down through the railing. She looked back at Quinn and took a step, closing the distance between them. His eyes held hers, sending a frisson of awareness up her spine. He lifted a hand slowly, brushing the backs of his fingers along her cheek. Sensation teemed within, flutters spinning wildly inside.

"What are we doing, Lace?" he asked, his voice a low murmur.

She could barely think for the feel of his subtle touch, yearning for more. "This," she said, her voice raspy. She stretched up, slipped her hand around his nape and tugged him down to meet her lips. The moment their lips met, she sighed in relief. Kissing Quinn was a strange, combustible mixture of familiar and unfamiliar. She knew him so well, yet she didn't know him like this at all. There was a fraction of hesitation from him, but when she traced along his lips with her tongue, he groaned and swept his tongue inside her mouth. She might be the one initiating these kisses, but he didn't hold back.

He fiercely claimed her mouth with bold strokes of his tongue in between nips and kisses. By the time his lips traveled from hers along her jawline, she was nearly vibrating with need. He nipped at her earlobe, sending hot shivers through her. She was plastered against him, aware of every inch of his muscled body flexing under her hands as she dragged one up along the corded muscles of his spine and the other stroking up under his t-shirt. His skin was warm, a contrast to the hardness of his body. Every inch of him was fit, and she savored the ripple of his muscles under her touch.

While she explored him, his hands meandered over her in turn, stroking down her spine to cup her bottom and tug her against him. She gasped when his lips made their way down along the column of her throat. He suddenly pulled back. The only sound was their breath heaving in the quiet room. She looked up to find him staring down at her. "Lace, I don't know if..."

She shook her head sharply. "Don't. Don't stop this." The force of her words surprised her.

Quinn stared down at her for several beats before moving swiftly. He stepped back, shrugged out of his jacket and toed off his boots. When Lacey realized he wasn't turning her down, she threw her jacket to the floor and kicked her shoes off. She began to turn toward him when he reached for her and lifted her in his arms, carrying her to the small couch. She slipped down when they reached the couch and looked up at him. She might be half out of her mind, but she wanted him, wanted this, so much it almost hurt. In the dim light, he lifted his hand again, tracing lightly along her jaw, down her neck, along her collarbone, down over the curve of her breast, and coming to rest in the dip of her waist.

With that reckless, wild edge spurring her along, she moved swiftly and hooked a hand under the hem of her shirt, pulling it up and over her head in one swoop. She flung it across the room. His breath came out in a hiss. He reached for her hands, stilling them in his. In that moment, she could feel his pulse beating against her palms, strong and fast. He dipped his head and brought his lips to hers again. They dove into another kiss—hot and fierce. The slow burn in her center had her arching and flexing into him, savoring the feel of his hard shaft against her low belly. Frantic to be closer and to feel more of him, she shoved his shirt up. He tore his lips free and reached behind his neck, pulling his shirt off in a single move to join hers in a rumple on the floor.

Impatient, Lacey yanked his jeans open and slipped her hand inside, stroking the length of his cock. Every time she tried to take over, he distracted her with his touch. His strong palm stroked over her belly and along the undersides of her breasts, his touch feather-light and sending hot shivers through her. He thumbed a nipple through the silk of her bra and leaned forward to lave it, dampening the silk and drawing the tight bead into his mouth. At her cry, he did the same to the other. She gripped his hair and gasped, a low moan breaking free. Hot liquid need built inside. She was drenched with desire and frantic to feel more of him, to lose herself in the wild longing pounding through her.

When he lifted his head and flicked his thumb under the clasp of her bra, she sighed at the feel of the cool air on her breasts. She was flushed all over, hot and bothered to the point of no return.

He traced her peaked nipples, his eyes following his touch. *"So beautiful. Lace, you have no idea what you do to me."*

His words came out on a breath, rough with desire. When she flicked her eyes up, his canted down. The dark desire in his slammed into her. That and something else, something deeper. For a flash, she lost the bold recklessness that had been driving her and became almost frightened. This was surreal, something she'd never thought she'd allow herself, and with Quinn, of all people. Yet, she'd blown too far past the barriers she'd kept in place to stop it. She shook her shoulders, letting her bra fall off and quickly shoved her jeans down before she had a chance to stop and think. His eyes followed every movement, never breaking away.

She paused to savor the sight of him, his muscled chest gleaming under the shadowed light from the loft. The smoky intensity in his gaze took her breath away. The air was alive around them, shimmering with the heat and desire arcing between them. She moved swiftly and shoved his jeans down, which he kicked free when she placed a palm on his chest and nearly shoved him down on the couch. Somehow, she felt marginally in control when she took over. She started to straddle him, but paused when he spoke.

"Lace."

She froze, one knee on the couch, and looked up at him.

"Hand me my jeans." He gestured to where they'd fallen just beyond her foot.

She leaned back and snagged them, puzzled at his request. In seconds, he pulled his wallet out of his back pocket and tossed a condom on the small table beside the couch. Oddly, the reality of what they were doing hit her when he did that. She experienced a glimmer of uncertainty, but she swatted it away. Whatever came of this, her longing for Quinn had only grown in its depth since she'd first felt its flicker.

She straddled him and stroked a hand in his hair. *"This is what I wanted the other night."* She sank her hips against him, savoring the feel of his hard cock against her, only the thin cotton of her panties and his briefs between them.

He gripped her hips and brought her down hard against him. *"This is what I wanted."*

He laced a hand in her hair and pulled her in for another kiss. She'd come to learn his kisses were pure art—the perfect blend of slow and fast, soft and hard, and so damn intoxicating they made her wild. By the time he pulled away, she was practically a puddle. Her hips were rolling, pleasure spiking from her core with each motion. His hand loosened in her hair and slid down her spine, every feather of his touch sending shivers across her skin. His touch curled around a hip and between her thighs, stroking across the damp cotton.

She didn't even recognize the sounds coming from her— pants, gasps, pleas and cries. He finally, finally pushed the cotton out of the way and delved into her folds, which were slick with need. He slid one finger inside her channel and then another. Her hips shifted restlessly, chasing after a peak she'd never climbed with anyone other than herself. Impatient she tugged at his briefs, shoving them far enough down to free his cock. Curling a palm around the velvety shaft, she glanced up when his breath came out in a rough groan. Still driving his fingers into and out of her channel in a slow circle, he fumbled for the condom with his other hand, making quick work of the foil packet and pushing her hand out of the way to roll it on.

In a blink, he was gripping her hip with one hand and positioning his cock at her entrance. Her channel throbbed with need. She'd been teetering on the edge of an orgasm for what felt like hours. Tonight had been one long episode of foreplay. His nearness was all her body needed to tune in and turn on, desire spinning it like a top.

"Lace, look at me..."

Lacey dragged her eyes open to find his waiting. Fire flashed in Quinn's gaze. He held her hips still for a hot moment, just long enough so that when he eased her down as he arched up, she almost came right then. Her eyes fell closed as she tumbled into the cauldron of sensation. He moved slowly and with purpose, each stroke seating him deeply within her. She rose and fell, her hips circling in time with him. The feel of him filling her was so intense, the pleasure built and built until she flew apart, sensation spinning loose inside as she cried out.

* * *

QUINN FELT Lacey's channel clench around him and opened his eyes to see her head fall back with a cry. She was utterly glorious in her release. As with everything, she threw herself into the moment, wild and abandoned. Once he decided he couldn't quite find it in himself to not allow this to happen, because he truly wanted it more than he'd wanted just about anything, he found himself overcome with pure need, a longing so deep it dragged him along with it.

He arched into her again, his own release thundering through him just as her head fell forward into the curve of his neck. She softened against him, and he eased his grip on her hips and slowly stroked a palm up her back to sift through her hair. They sat like that for so long, he lost track of time until he felt her skin prickle with goose bumps. It filtered into his awareness that it was chilly in her cabin.

"Hey, we should start a fire," he said softly.

She slowly lifted her head and met his eyes. His heart thumped, hard, and a wash of feeling rolled through him.

CHAPTER 7

*L*acey burrowed closer to Quinn. Half asleep, she didn't initially register what she doing, it felt *soooo* good to be curled up against him. He emanated heat and strength even in his sleep. As her brain started to become more aware, she flushed straight through. Oh. My. God. What had she done?

Her mind was swift with its reply. *You had the best sex. Ever. With Quinn. So good, you forgot to lose your mind over it last night. Maybe you should do that now.*

Lacey lay still, unable to bring herself to move away from Quinn. They were tangled together. Her head was tucked against his shoulder with his arm curled over hers, holding her close against him. She could feel the muscled planes of his chest and the steady beat of his heart under her palm. Her leg was thrown across his. They were completely naked. Just lying still with his glorious, purely masculine self beside her, it was as if a switch was flicked in her body. Heat suffused her, her low belly clenched and *holy hell* did she want him with a fierceness that took her breath away.

The reckless edge that had pushed her to be so bold last

night had faded in the gray light of dawn. Those hours of being close to him at dinner and a few glasses of wine had knocked away her usual reserve and her sanity. Yet, what she'd anticipated didn't even come close to how amazing it felt to be with him. After generally concluding sex didn't seem to spin her top the way it did for others, she now realized she just hadn't had it with Quinn yet. Even without that reckless edge, she wanted Quinn and it wasn't just sex. She felt half-crazy. She'd never thought she'd be one to want the whole commitment thing. Heck, she didn't really even do casual. Her attempts at dating had been few and far between. She'd envisioned herself as carrying on with her life of independence and free from the trials and tribulations of love. Then, Quinn had walked off that plane in Anchorage, her old friend who'd never elicited even a twinge of desire from her, and her body and heart had sat up, as if in a coma all those years, and taken notice.

Quinn shifted in his sleep, his palm sliding off her shoulder and down along her spine in a sleepy caress. A shiver chased behind his touch, her skin prickling with awareness. He mumbled something and then cleared his throat. Lacey froze. She didn't know how to face him this morning. Her mind started spinning, wondering what last night had been like for him, wondering how he viewed her and what he might want, and worrying she'd gone and done the dumbest thing ever by not only giving in to her reckless desire, but insisting on it. She was saved from further mental gymnastics when he spoke.

"Mmm. Mornin'."

She wracked her brain trying to think of what to say when it occurred to her it was quite simple. "Good morning," she mumbled into his shoulder. That's all she had to say, something normal. Maybe if she acted normal, she'd feel normal.

She felt Quinn shift and angle his body toward her. They

were already twined together, but he was flat on his back. He slowly pushed up on his elbow, the hand on her back sliding lower as he did. She managed to open her eyes and found his warm amber gaze on her. His hair was tousled. Before she even realized what she was doing, she reached up and sifted her fingers through the straight locks. His mouth curled at one corner.

"That bad, huh?" His voice was gravelly with sleep, though his eyes were alert and assessing.

She bit her lip and let her hand fall where it landed on his chest. She couldn't seem to not touch him. She shrugged. "Not really."

He was quiet for a long moment before he lifted his hand and brushed her hair back away from her face. He dipped his head and kissed her quickly before sliding his arm out from under her and sitting up. He glanced toward the front windows beyond the loft railing. She pushed herself up, tugging the sheet with her and wrapping it over her chest. Even though Quinn was more than familiar with her breasts at this point, she wasn't used to waking up with someone.

He glanced to her, the corner of his mouth curling in a grin again when he saw her with the sheet tucked under her arms. "It snowed last night," he said.

She forgot her embarrassment as she leaned up to glance over the railing. She loved the first snow every year. The landscape outside looked as if it had been coated in fairy dust. A thin layer of snow covered the field and spruce trees. It wasn't fully light yet and slightly overcast. "The first snow is my favorite," she said softly.

When she glanced away from the windows, Quinn was watching her. She flushed and then flushed even deeper when she felt the heat on her cheeks. He saved her by flipping the covers off and standing. Her mouth went dry. Dear God. He was a dangerously gorgeous specimen of man.

Every inch of him was honed, hard muscle. He looked so good, she wanted to spread butter on him for breakfast. Entirely unself-conscious, he walked to the bathroom adjacent to her bedroom and leaned against the doorframe. She swallowed at the sight of his arousal.

"I'm guessing we should maybe talk about whether you're hoping to keep this private for now. Because if I don't get back to the lodge soon, everyone there will know I spent the night here," he said, watching her carefully.

Oh. Right. She hadn't even thought about that possibility. Her mind started to whirr, and she shook her head sharply. She didn't really care if anyone wondered about her and Quinn. She had enough going on without adding another worry to her mental list. She wasn't ready to blare it to the world because she didn't know what she would blare, but she wasn't up for cloak and dagger and trying to hide things.

"It doesn't matter," she said with a shrug.

His eyes widened and he arched a brow in question. "Are you sure?"

"It's too much work to try to hide anything around here, so it'll just stress me out. If anyone asks, we can say you walked me back and crashed here. That's enough."

"Okay then. Mind if I shower?"

"Go ahead. Want some pancakes?" She knew Quinn loved pancakes, and she couldn't help herself from wanting to make something he'd like.

"Absolutely! Wait for me to make the coffee though," he said over his shoulder as he stepped into the bathroom.

"Fine," she called out. "I can make decent coffee too, you know."

"Mine's better," he replied over the running water.

* * *

EARLY THAT AFTERNOON, Quinn turned out of the lodge driveway and drove toward town. Once the sun broke through the clouds, it had melted the snow, leaving a glittering landscape behind with drops of water glistening on the trees. He marveled at the view as he drove down the winding hill to downtown Diamond Creek. Like most coastal towns in this part of Alaska, the town was nestled against the foothills of the mountains surrounding it. He had a clear view of Kachemak Bay and the mountains on its far side for his entire drive into town. He was on his way to his interview with Dr. Daniels, but his mind was filled with thoughts of Lacey.

Last night had been, well, flat out mind-blowing. He'd known ever since he'd laid eyes on her that Lacey was beautiful and so damn sexy with her combination of femininity and tomboyishness. Beautiful and sexy didn't even come close to capturing what it had been like with her last night. She was bold, reckless and wild, tempered with a refreshing lack of artifice. It had taken more discipline than he thought he had this morning to keep from rolling atop her this morning and sinking inside of her. The only thing that held him back was not wanting to push too far and too fast. He sensed she was taken aback by what had happened, even though she'd been the instigator. Against reason, he couldn't have turned her away last night no matter what. Now, he had to figure out how to make a path forward with her without scaring her off.

He couldn't quite believe what had happened, nor could he quite believe his train of thought. Between college, medical school, and his many travel excursions, he hadn't had much time to consider the idea of romantic attachments. He'd never been opposed to the idea, per se, but it hadn't been a priority. When he'd made plans to return home to Alaska, it had been in the back of his mind that he might finally be in a place where he could think about something other than casual when it came to women. Yet, he hadn't expected Lacey. The moment he'd laid eyes on her when she met him at the airport, which she'd done many times over the years when they ran trips together, the desire that flickered to life in her eyes was like a match to flame for him.

It felt as if events between them were spinning beyond his control. Because the last thing he'd expected was for her to be the aggressor. Yet, he should've known better. Lacey didn't do anything in half-measures. His mind flashed to the feel of her channel clenching around him, every inch of her plastered against him, and he had to take a deep breath and talk his body down. He shook his head sharply. He needed to get his mind off of Lacey and onto his upcoming interview.

Not much later, Quinn stood up from his chair and held a hand out to Dr. Daniels. "Thank you. It's been great to talk with you. Please call if..."

Dr. Daniels, a thin, spry older man with pure white hair and a lanky frame, gave him a firm shake and shook his head, cutting into what Quinn was saying. "No need to call. I've already decided. If you'd like to be the doctor who takes over this practice, just say when," he said firmly.

Quinn's surprise must have shown on his face because Dr. Daniels chuckled, his blue eyes twinkling in his weathered face. "I knew before you showed up here, I'd be willing to hire you when it came to your background and knowledge. I just needed to meet you to make sure you'd be a good fit for the community. Harvard looks great on paper, but not so much if you can't shake the arrogant suit and tie act. You're about as down to earth as it gets. Plus, Donna likes you," he said with another laugh, referring to the office manager who been his main employee for over two decades.

"Well, that's a mark in my favor," Quinn replied. He took a breath and nodded. "I wouldn't have applied if I didn't want this opportunity, so I'll go ahead and say yes. I'll need a few weeks to take care of some logistical details, but after that, I can start whenever you're ready."

Dr. Daniels smiled widely and clapped him on the shoulder. "Just tell me when you'll be here. As you know, I've scaled back on my appointments, but we have a backlog of people waiting for you to get here. I can hold them off for a few weeks though."

Moments later, Quinn climbed into his truck, almost stunned at how easily that went. He meant what he said—he wanted the position and he wanted to be in Diamond Creek. Yet now that it was imminent, his mind was spinning with the implications of what it would mean to be in proximity to Lacey all the time. Before the idea had been unrealized, so it was a 'what if' scenario. Now, it was something else altogether. He wanted her with a ferocity he'd never experienced. When he pulled out onto the highway, he went in the direction of the harbor. He could use a chilly walk on the beach.

CHAPTER 8

After Quinn left, Lacey threw on her running clothes, jumped in her car and drove to her favorite beach for a long run. Though she loved summers in Alaska, she loved it even more when the weather turned chilly and left miles and miles of empty beaches. After walking down a short path through drooping tall grasses, faded and well past their time, she stepped onto the beach. This particular stretch of coastline wasn't formally named, but she'd called it Raven's Beach since she was a little girl. She and Marley had come down here for a walk with their mother once and found a group of ravens frolicking in the air by a nearby bluff. She'd never seen as many ravens as they saw that day, but she always saw a few here. They nested in the cluster of spruce trees atop the bluff.

She loved this beach because at the right time of year, one could feel as if they were all alone in the world. The beach itself wasn't too far from downtown Diamond Creek, yet the curve of the coastline hid the town from view here. The beach overlooked Kachemak Bay with Mount Augustine, one of several nearby volcanoes, standing sentry in the distance in Cook Inlet. The pristine waters and breath-taking views were what made Diamond Creek one of Alaska's coastal jewels. This beach exemplified the beauty with the ocean sparkling under the sun, a glacier glowing bright in the distance and the mountains rising high in jagged peaks on the far side of the bay. She took in a gulp of the salty air and shivered when a gust of wind blasted off the water.

She began running, starting slow for a few minutes before picking up her pace. She loved the freedom she experienced when she ran. She thrived on pushing herself to her limit until her body was up against its own endurance. A sense of transcendence flooded her whenever she ran so hard that she finally stopped, her breath heaving and pure exhaustion washing through her. That's how far and fast she pushed herself today until she reached the curve of the coastline where a stream cascaded down the bluff to the beach, the clear water rolling over the rocks and slipping into the ocean. Her breath misted in the cool air. Though the snow had melted after this morning, the sun had merely taken the nip off the cold. Autumn was being chased away by the authority of winter.

As her breath slowed, she rested her hands on her hips and stared out over the ocean. Quinn strolled into her thoughts. Well, stroll didn't quite cut it. He strode in the way he walked, with confidence and ease. All day long, she'd shied away from thinking about him. Somehow, she'd managed to behave normally with him this morning. She'd made pancakes and he'd made his amazing coffee. She'd loved every minute of last night and savored every minute of this morning because it felt so...good. Just good. There was a reason they'd stayed friends over the years, though time and distance could have allowed their friendship to fade. Quinn was easy to be around—funny with a sly touch, warm and kind. Oh, and sexy as all hell. How she ever missed that glaringly obvious detail, she would never know. It wasn't that she didn't notice he was objectively handsome, she'd just never felt that zing with him. It was most definitely a zing now.

She was all a muddle in her head and had no clue how to handle her feelings. There was their friendship and then there was last night, a blazing conflagration of passion and intense connection. Oh, and the most amazing orgasm she'd ever had. There was that. With a shake of her head, she turned away and started to jog back. The tide was coming in, inching closer along the damp sand. Her eyes tracked the waves rolling into the shore, the rhythmic sound soothing her. She was within sight of the short path leading to her car when she felt a wave of weakness. She tried to push through it because that's how she always pushed through, but she couldn't. One of her knees gave out, and she stumbled, falling to her knees on the sand.

She tried to push up with her hands, but she didn't have it. A flash of panic rose within. She closed her eyes and took several deep breaths to ease the feeling. Her strength and her energy, two qualities she'd always had in spades, failed her completely. She eased onto her hips and sat in the sand. With this now being the fourth time she'd felt like this, she was becoming somewhat familiar with the experience and she hated it. She was clinging to the idea that nothing was really wrong, but in the middle of another moment like this, it was hard to hold onto that idea. She was relieved to find her vision wasn't blurry, although her eyes felt tired and droopy. She stared out over the water and kept breathing. The wind gusted off the bay, blowing a loose lock of her hair across her eyes. Even lifting her hand to brush it out of the way took an enormous amount of energy.

After several minutes, she thought she had it in her to stand, so she carefully knelt and rose on one foot. When she was standing, she started to walk, but she was so tired. So, so tired. She reached a piece of driftwood, an old, faded tree lying on its side in the sand, and carefully sat again. The path to her car was maybe a quarter of a mile away, but the distance yawned in front of her. The wind was picking up, coming in steady from across the bay and sending shivers through her. She'd worn a lightweight windbreaker over her fitted running jersey, but it wasn't much if she wasn't moving and building up her internal heat. Resigned, she fumbled in her pocket for her smartphone and pulled it out. She sat there for several moments, torn between calling Marley or Quinn. If she called Marley, there'd be a lot more explaining to do. She knew she needed to talk to Marley and her parents, but she wasn't quite up for it just now. She tapped the screen and pulled up Quinn's number.

He answered on the first ring. "Hey Lace, calling to check on my interview?" he asked. She could hear the grin in his question, and it made her smile.

"Maybe. How'd it go?" she countered, relieved for a moment to ignore the reason she was calling.

"I'll be the new doctor at Coastal Medical Clinic within the month."

"That's awesome! I knew it!" For a moment, she completely forgot why she'd called. Joy rose within. She was genuinely happy for him and elated to know he'd be here—close to her. On the heels of her temporary insanity, she reminded herself she didn't know what the hell she was doing with Quinn and she could barely walk right now.

Quinn chuckled. "Maybe you were confident, but I was just hopeful. Anyway, I was heading back to the lodge. You up for a hike this afternoon?"

A perfectly expected question from him. When they weren't guiding trips in the backcountry together and happened to be in the same area, they often took off on short hikes together and with other friends. Anxiety knotted in her chest. She didn't like feeling the way she did.

At all. Even worse, she didn't like feeling this vulnerable. She didn't want to have him see her weak like this again. She felt tossed asunder in the confusion of her attraction and the intimacy she'd experienced with him last night.

She could and would push through this. She tried again to stand and managed it, but just barely. Hot tears pressed against the back of her eyes and her throat tightened. Shit, shit, shit. A flash of anger rose inside. She was infuriated to realize the weakness wasn't fading like she hoped. She wanted to fight back against it, but she couldn't. There was no way around this. She was going to have to ask for help.

"Lace, you there?" Quinn asked into the too long pause.

She eased back down onto the driftwood and swallowed against the tears welling. "Yeah, I'm here. Um, I…uh…might need your help, and a hike's probably not gonna happen today."

She could practically see him shift into serious. She'd seen him spring into action when emergencies happened in the backcountry. Just like she was, he'd been a certified Wilderness First Responder for years. When something went awry, his teasing manner disappeared and he acted quickly and with confidence. "What happened?"

She took another breath, letting it out on a sigh. "I went for a run on that beach I took you to a few years back. I felt great at first, but that weird weakness thing happened. It's not going away, and I'm not so sure I can make it all the way back to my car."

"Remind me how to get there," he said, his words clipped.

Lacey quickly gave him directions. Quinn insisted on keeping her on the phone while he drove to meet her, which annoyed her to no end, but she didn't hang up. He ran through a series of questions while she simply kept repeating that her legs felt weak and one of them was tingling. Minutes later, she saw him running through the fallen down grass and onto the beach. She marveled at how swiftly he reached her when it seemed like it would take her forever to walk from where she sat to the path to her car. He stopped in front of her and knelt down, his eyes coasting over her. She'd managed to get a handle on the tears threatening, which was a relief.

"Hey," she said, trying to smile but barely pulling it off. She slipped her phone in her pocket and looked up at him.

"How're you feeling now?"

"Just the way I said I was a minute or so ago," she replied, annoyed at his repetitive questions. "I'm sure it will pass, but it's chilly and the tide's coming in, and I didn't know how long it would take me to try to walk to the damn car myself."

Quinn nodded slowly and sat down on the log beside her. He stared out over the water. "Let's get going, but we're going to see your doctor, and it's not up for debate. You can't keep ignoring this."

Too tired to argue with him and so relieved he was here, she nodded. "Okay."

A strong gust of wind blasted across the water, and she shivered. He glanced to her. "Let's go."

He stood and held a hand out as he positioned himself to her side. With him gripping one hand tightly and pulling her up while he eased his arm around her waist, standing was much easier. He glanced to her, as if gauging how she was doing, before starting to walk slowly. With his strength to lean on, walking was far less exhausting. It wasn't too long before they were standing beside his SUV. He was quiet as he helped her into the passenger seat.

"Need anything from your car?" he asked.

"Oh yes! My purse is in there."

"Got your keys?"

She tugged them out of her jacket pocket and handed them over. He closed the door, leaving her alone in the quiet car. It occurred to her it should tell her a lot about how she felt that she didn't even consider driving. She was just too weak. She was starting to bounce back and the tingling in her leg had disappeared, but she didn't have it in her to try to drive home, or to even argue about going to the doctor with Quinn.

* * *

QUINN WALKED beside Lacey into her cabin. She'd surprised him by not arguing about going to see her doctor, which gave him the opportunity to meet the only other doctor in Diamond Creek, Dr. Rita Marshall. Lacey clearly felt comfortable with her, so he was relieved for that. He hadn't been too focused on the professional aspect of meeting Dr. Marshall, although he was pleased to find her gracious and kind. She already knew he'd accepted the position from Dr. Daniels and had explained there were more than enough patients to share, so competition wasn't a concern.

He was feeling caught in the middle with Lacey. He had his own ideas about what might help, but he knew he was far from objective. He was beyond relieved with Dr. Marshall's approach. She'd prescribed a brief regimen of corticosteroids and made a referral for another MRI. She hadn't allowed Lacey to leave without an injection to start her medication and scheduled Lacey for a check up within the week. Lacey had been quiet on the drive home. He was so stirred up inside, he was relieved for the silence. Before last night and before the lightning hot attraction between them had gone from an idea to reality, he'd have been worried for her. Now, he was wrestling with a powerful need to protect her. He didn't want to leave her alone tonight, but he wasn't so sure how she'd feel about that.

Once they were in her cabin, Lacey eyed the woodstove. "I should probably start a fire."

83

He glanced from her to the woodstove and back again. "I'll take care of it if that's okay."

She chewed her lip and stared at him for a long moment. Her auburn hair was tied back in a ponytail. Between the wind and her run, many locks had fallen loose. Her freckles stood out against her pale skin. Even tired, she was beautiful. He shackled the urge to pull her into his arms.

"That'd be great," she finally said. "Mind if I take a shower? I'm all clammy from running and then getting cold on the beach."

"Of course not. You shower, and I'll get a fire going."

She turned and started to walk to the stairs.

"Hey, promise you'll call out if you feel weak again," he said.

She stopped at the foot of the stairs and looked over at him. She rolled her eyes, which let him know she was feeling better. "Promise. But I'm actually feeling a little better. That shot Dr. Marshall gave me is already helping."

"Good. I think you'd have been feeling better anyway, but the corticosteroids should help with the inflammation that triggered this."

She grinned. "You just can't help talking like a doctor."

He shrugged. "It's what I do. Now go get in the shower and warm up."

Once he heard the water running, he stepped onto the front porch where he'd seen a rack full of chopped wood. He carried an armful inside and quickly laid the logs in the woodstove and started a fire. By the time Lacey came downstairs, the heat was beginning to filter through the chilly cabin air. His breath caught when he saw her. Her cheeks were rosy, and her jade eyes were luminous in her face. She wore a pair of sweatpants that hugged her curvy hips and emphasized her strong thighs before they flared out, swinging around her ankles as she walked. She'd topped those with a fitted t-shirt and a sweatshirt that hung open, leaving a way too tempting view of her breasts. He had to force his eyes away and focus on her face as she made her way to him where he stood by the kitchen counter.

"Much better," Lacey said as she reached the counter and pulled a stool out to sit. "Whatcha doing?"

"Waiting for the water to boil." He pointed to the kettle starting to hum to the stove.

She grinned. "What for?"

"I figured something hot was called for. Coffee, tea, hot chocolate, or something else?"

She cocked her head to the side, her smile widening. "Hot chocolate."

"You're gonna have to tell me where to find it," he replied, smiling widely. His relief at seeing her back to herself was palpable.

After he served her some hot chocolate and made some coffee for himself, he joined her at the counter. She took a slow swallow and sighed. "Delicious. I finally feel normal again." She paused, tracing the edge of the counter with her fingertip. Her hair fell in a tousle around her shoulders when she looked up at him. "I'm really glad you got the job," she said softly. "I didn't mean to derail your afternoon like this."

"I'm glad you called me." His chest tightened at his words, realizing what it must've said about how she felt that she called for help. Lacey wasn't much for asking for help. He couldn't recall any other time she'd needed it, save her two falls during their Katmai trip.

"Maybe we should order takeout to celebrate. I'd say we should go out, but I'm too tired for that. We'll have to save that for another night," she said, her voice interrupting his thoughts.

"Works for me. What do you want?"

"You pick. We're celebrating your new job. For takeout options, if we pick up, we have more choices. If we want delivery, it's Glacier Pizza. That's the only place in town that delivers."

"Glacier Pizza it is."

Lacey slipped off her stool and walked to the counter on the other side. Opening a drawer, she pulled out a menu and tossed it to him.

CHAPTER 9

*L*acey jogged up the steps to her parents' house, pausing on the deck to look out over the field. Snow had fallen again last night, leaving the landscape sparkling where the sun struck it and melted the thin layer of snow. She scanned the horizon, her eyes traveling along the peaks and valleys of the mountains across the bay. Her childhood home was only minutes from the small cabin where she was staying. It was lower down the hill toward town and had a more open view of the bay. She knew the view by heart. At the moment, she needed the comfort of the familiar.

She'd slept in Quinn's arms last night, although nothing other than that happened. Oddly, the intimacy of being close to him like that after him witnessing her hardly able to walk again made her feel vulnerable. She'd woken beside him and wanted to stay there all day. Her body had betrayed her again with need thrumming through her, but she'd shoved it away. He must've sensed something because even though she could feel the hard, hot length of him against her leg, seeing as she woke plastered to his side, he benignly offered to make coffee when she leapt out of bed and practically ran for the shower.

He'd left to run a few errands in town and go back to the lodge. She'd promised herself she'd talk to her mother this morning. Even if this 'whatever' she had going on didn't turn out to be MS, she knew she needed to cue her family in, although it grated on her to consider it. Talking about it made it seem as if something would come of it. If it weren't for Quinn being around yesterday, she'd have needed to call one of them. She turned away from the view and gave a quick knock on the kitchen door before stepping inside.

"Hey Mom!"

"Upstairs, hon. I'll be down in a minute. Help yourself to coffee or tea," her mother called out.

Lacey hung her jacket on the coatrack by the door and kicked off her running shoes. Her mother had a fresh pot of coffee ready, so Lacey poured herself a cup and sat down at the small round table by the windows. Growing up, their home had always been a bustle of activity between her and Marley and their various activities. While Marley had various computers and projects strewn about the house, Lacey's sports gear was scattered in a trail behind wherever she went. Her father was gone for a few weeks on another fishing trip. He used to fish more frequently when they were younger, but now he only went once a year. At the sound of footsteps coming down the stairs, she glanced over to see her mother walking into the kitchen.

Holly Adams smiled warmly and stepped to the booth to drop a kiss on Lacey's cheek. "Hello dear." She moved past Lacey and poured herself a cup of tea before joining Lacey at the table. Lacey and Marley had inherited their mother's auburn hair and green eyes. Holly's hair was streaked with silver now, but her green eyes were as bright as they'd ever been.

"How're things at the hospital?" Lacey asked, figuring

she'd start with the usuals. Holly had been a nurse at the local hospital for many years. She'd decreased her work schedule in the last few, but Lacey wasn't so sure her mother could ever stand to retire. She genuinely loved her job and was beloved by residents for her kind manner at the hospital.

Holly took a sip of coffee and shrugged. "Same, same. Busy as always. There was a car accident on the highway outside of town last night, so I worked late. Four teens with one of them driving way too fast. Thank goodness they're all going to be okay!"

"Good to know. I'm sure they got your little lecture on driving," Lacey said with a wry grin.

Holly chuckled. "I decided to save it for today when they're feeling a bit better. Anyway, how are you? I saw your car yesterday at Raven's Beach and figured you must've gone for a run."

Lacey grinned. She loved that her mother had adopted her childhood name of the beach. As she considered how her afternoon had gone there, her grin faded. She needed to just get this off her chest. She took a deep breath and eyed her mother.

Holly's eyes narrowed. "Are you okay?"

"Well, I suppose it depends. I came by today because I thought you needed to know I've had some medical issues recently, including yesterday when I went for a run."

Her mother's eyes widened, and she angled her head to the side. "Please tell me you're okay."

"Mom, obviously I'm okay. Look at me. I'm sitting right here, completely fine. I wasn't sure about talking to you sooner because I didn't know if it was necessary. So here's what happened..."

She quickly summarized the events in Katmai, her subsequent visit to the hospital in Anchorage, and then what happened yesterday afternoon. When she got to the end and looked over at her mother, her chest tightened and she had to swallow against the lump in her throat. Her mother looked so concerned. Making it even harder, she didn't scold Lacey for not telling her sooner, although Lacey knew she might be just about biting her tongue off at that.

"Maybe I should've said something sooner, but I don't think anything will come of it. The doctor in Anchorage said sometimes people never have another episode, and Quinn said the same thing. After he came to get me yesterday, he made me promise to talk to you soon. I was going to anyway, but it's just... I don't know, I didn't know what to say. I just hate it. I don't like feeling weak and I want it to go away."

Holly looked at her thoughtfully and took a sip of coffee. "Even if it's MS, you don't need to turn it into more than it is. I completely understand it would be frightening, especially for you..."

Lacey cut her off. "Why especially for me?"

Her mother's gaze softened and she reached across the table to squeeze Lacey's hand. "Because you're Brawny. Ever since you two gave each other those nicknames, you've lived up to it. I don't think you rely on your strength and daredevil spirit because of a silly nickname, but I do think the name stuck when you were kids because it fit so perfectly. The way your strength defines you, it's probably a bit more scary to feel weak out of the blue that like." Her mother paused, her eyes considering. "You might need to think about the fact that this might not go away."

Lacey stared at her mother, a panicky feeling rising inside. In the short time since she'd experienced any of what was going on, she'd been mentally kicking and screaming. She didn't want to have to think about any possibility other than this whole thing becoming a surreal memory. She forced herself to take a breath and looked over at her mother. She didn't want to argue because she knew it would only worry her mother. Instead, she took a sip of coffee and nodded slowly, striving to be nonchalant. "Maybe, but I don't see any point in thinking the worst right now. I'll wait and see."

Her mother's perceptive gaze held hers. If her mother thought it was worth arguing her point, she decided against it. "Well, be that as it may, don't you dare keep hiding this from us. If Quinn hadn't been there yesterday, what would you have done?"

"I would've called you or Marley. I really would have. It's just he was here, and he already knew what might be going on, so it was easier to call him."

Holly was quiet for several beats before nodding slowly and shifting gears. "What did Dr. Marshall think?"

A few days ago, it would have bothered Lacey to no end to have to answer questions about what her doctor thought, but at the moment, it was a bit of a relief. The emotional weight of trying to talk about it was too close for comfort, so focusing on the dry, medical details seemed easier somehow.

A little bit later, after her mother hugged her tightly at the door, Lacey started her walk back to her cabin. As she threaded her way through the trees, her phone chirped. A look at the screen showed a text from Marley.

Where are you? Your car's here, so I know you're somewhere nearby. I stopped by to see if you wanted to grab some lunch. It's freezing out, so I'm waiting inside.

Lacey picked up her pace a little bit and quickly tapped out her reply.

Walking back right now. See you in a few.

Within a few minutes, she was jogging up the steps to her cabin. Marley opened the door to greet her.

"Hey there!"

"Hey yourself," Lacey replied, stepping inside and closing the door behind her.

Marley and Gage's daughter Holly was on the couch gnawing on her tattered stuffed parrot. Lacey stepped to the couch and ran her fingers through Holly's soft hair before dropping a kiss on her forehead. "Hey little miss, nice to see you."

Holly stared up at Lacey with her wide green eyes and gurgled something impossible to interpret with the parrot in her mouth. Lacey laughed softly and plunked down on the couch beside her.

"Lunch would be perfect. Where do you wanna go?"

"The Boathouse is having locals specials all week," Marley replied.

"Let's go then." Lacey stood and leaned over to lift Holly into her arms.

After the short drive into town, Lacey carried Holly as they walked into the Boathouse Café. The café was in a renovated diner that retained its original warm feel. The diner counter had been updated with polished mahogany and served as a bar. The kitchen grill was visible to one side of the bar with copper cookware hanging above. The booths and tables were also polished wood with a variety of rich colored curtains adding brightness to the space. Once they were seated and Holly was settled in her high chair, Lacey looked out over the bay. With the café situated on a bluff by the ocean, the view here was phenomenal. Clouds obscured the sun from this morning now with wind scudding across the water and leaving the surface choppy.

After they ordered, Lacey looked over at Marley and contemplated whether she was up for a replay of her conversation with her mother earlier. She decided she'd rather get it over with than delay further.

"You know how you asked if I was okay last week?"

Marley had been adjusting the tray on the high chair and swung her eyes to Lacey, her gaze sharp and perceptive. "Of course. Something's up. I tried to pry it out of Quinn, but he wasn't much help. Spill it."

Lacey experienced a flash of gratitude for the kind of friend Quinn was. With a deep breath, she repeated everything she'd discussed with her mother earlier, including the doctor's visits. When she was done, she looked over at Marley. Marley's face was tight and her eyes concerned.

"Why didn't you say something sooner?" Marley shook her head sharply. "Scratch that. I know exactly why you didn't say something sooner. You're the badass of the family, so this must be driving you nuts. What did Dr. Marshall say? When will you know if this is something more?"

Lacey sighed. "Same thing as the doctor in Anchorage. It annoys the hell out of me everyone keeps saying this is still one episode, but Quinn says it's because an episode can last weeks or more. I did a little internet research, which Quinn said is not the best idea, but anyway, some people wait years before they're formally diagnosed with MS because there has to be more than one episode and they have to confirm nerve damage in more than one location. Whatever. All I know is this sucks. Either way, I'm pretty sure this is all just gonna fade into nothing."

Their waiter arrived at that moment and delivered their drinks and an appetizer of mini halibut tacos. He also filled Holly's small cup with water before departing. Lacey quickly transferred several of the tiny halibut tacos onto her plate before pushing the rest over to Marley. They ate quietly for a few minutes before Marley spoke again.

"I don't really know what to say. I want to tell you not to worry, but I'd be worried as hell."

Lacey took a sip of her water to wash down a bite of food and nodded. "I'm focusing on the fact there's a good chance it's nothing." Now that she'd managed to get these uncomfortable conversations over with, she didn't want to dwell. There wasn't much else to say and talking about it sent anxiety churning through her. "Mind if we move on now that I got that off my chest. I should've said something sooner, but I guess I was wishing it would all go away. Hopefully it still will, but for now, there's not much else to say."

Marley held her gaze for a long moment, her eyes warm and concerned. "I suppose you're right." Her expression softened and she smiled slyly. "Maybe you could tell me what's up with Quinn."

Lacey felt her cheeks heat and damned her tendency to blush. With their fair skin and auburn hair, she and Marley were both blushers. She was about to say something when their waiter arrived again, this time serving their salmon burgers and sweet potato fries, along with a tiny grilled cheese sandwich for Holly. The interruption distracted Lacey enough that she wasn't flushed straight through when she finally looked over at Marley again.

Marley grinned, her eyes gleaming with mischief. "You wanted to change the subject, so I did." She paused to put a bite-sized piece of Holly's grilled cheese sandwich back on its plate. Holly promptly grabbed it and stuffed the tiny piece in her mouth. "So, back to Quinn. He doesn't seem to be staying at the lodge, so I thought maybe you could tell me where he's been. Gage said he saw him walking back on the trail that goes to your cabin this morning."

Lacey rolled her eyes, trying to beat back the flush washing through her. It wasn't just the twinge of embarrassment, but also the fact she could hardly think about Quinn without getting hot and bothered. "Fine. He might have stayed with me." She'd told herself she didn't care if anyone wondered what was up with them. In a way she didn't, but she was rattled by how confused she was about her own feelings. If there was anyone she could talk to about it, Marley was that person. Lacey shoved down her embarrassment and looked at Marley. "I don't know what's up with us. Ever since he came back, it's been…different. I'd rather not go into details, but let's just say something happened. Now, I'm all freaked out because you know me, I don't do relationships. I like to do my own thing. But Quinn's my friend and now I'm worried we might have messed that up. I don't know what he wants and… Ugh. I don't know. I could use some advice."

Marley cocked her head and smiled softly. "Something happening between you and Quinn doesn't surprise me. I always thought he was the perfect guy for you. Have you talked at all?"

Lacey couldn't quite bring herself to admit to Marley she'd been the one to push the envelope first that night in the hotel in Anchorage. His words echoed in her mind. *"...there's no way in hell I'm having a one off night with you..."* She'd been too busy fumbling with her attraction to him at the moment that she hadn't explored that further. Since then and especially since the other night when they'd gone far past a kiss, she kept replaying his words in her mind, wondering what he meant. On the surface, she knew what he meant, but she didn't have the bigger picture. Did it mean he wanted more? Or just that he didn't want to let sex get in the way of their friendship?

"Not really. Even worse than not knowing what he wants, I don't know what I want. I don't have much experience with relationships. Well, I don't do them. I thought maybe you'd have some ideas because, well, you have more experience in this area than I do."

Marley's eyes widened. "Um, aside from Gage, I'm not exactly an expert. All I did for ten years after college was work and date once in a blue moon. But, I do know you won't figure out anything without talking about it. Quinn's a great guy. It's not like he's going to be a jerk about it. If my guess is right, he's had a thing for you for years."

"What?!"

Marley grinned widely. "Uh huh. I'm not blind, but you are. I never said anything because you didn't seem to think of him any way other than as a friend."

Lacey was reeling from Marley's lighthearted observation, which must have showed on her face because Marley's grin faded as she shook her head. "So you never noticed Quinn might have wanted something more than being your hiking buddy? Seriously?"

"Seriously. Why would you even think that?"

"Because of the way he looked at you. It wasn't blatant, but it was always there. Maybe I'm wrong, but I don't think so. Now that you've actually let something happen, maybe you should ask him. I might not know him as well as you do, but I know he doesn't like to lie. He was not pleased with having to cover for you when I asked if something happened when you were in Katmai."

Lacey took another bite of her salmon burger, thoughts tumbling through her mind. If Quinn had been into her all these years, how could she have missed it? Marley, being her usual perceptive self, read Lacey's mind.

"You're wondering how you didn't notice. It's because you just don't pay attention to men. You're every guy's friend, but you don't think about men as anything other than friends. Not that it's my business, but you're so tough, it's like you can't let yourself be anything else. I love how badass you are, so don't go thinking you need to change, but it wouldn't hurt to broaden your horizons. If something could really be there for you and Quinn, you couldn't find a better guy. He's not intimidated by your badassery, he could care less that you might be better than him at a few things, and he's just an all around good guy. On top of all that, now he's officially moving here," Marley said with a firm nod, her eyes twinkling.

Lacey, still trying to absorb the idea she'd somehow missed Quinn's attraction to her sooner, finished off her salmon burger and leaned back in her chair. "Okay, whether or not Quinn's had a thing for me all this time, you still haven't given me any advice. What do I do now?"

Marley chuckled. "I think the only thing you can do is talk to him. Trust me, I know it's not easy. Gage was the first guy I was ever really into and it's pretty scary to care that much." She paused and looked over at Lacey. "You also might want to try to figure out what you want. Do you want something more with him? Or just more great sex?"

A flush raced through Lacey, heating her neck and face again. "Did I say anything about great sex?" she asked with a roll of her eyes.

"You didn't have to. I can tell," Marley said with a sly grin.

CHAPTER 10

Quinn reached the top of the slope and paused to catch his breath beside a small ski hut, likely used for first aid and sundry needs up on the mountain during winter. He put his hands on his hips and turned in a slow circle. Last Frontier Lodge was situated at the base of the tallest peak in the area, offering a three hundred and sixty degree view. He scanned the nearby peaks and spun around to see Kachemak Bay in the distance. Two volcanoes were visible as well. Mount Augustine stood closer in the waters of Cook Inlet, the ocean inlet that led from the Pacific Ocean inland into Alaska and fed several small bays. Mount Illiamna was further in the distance. Mount Augustine was known for its occasional eruptions, spewing ash all over Southcentral Alaska and disrupting flights.

Quinn had once joined a biologist friend for a trip to Mount Augustine. He'd been in awe of how it felt to be on a volcano in the middle of the ocean. He turned to face the lodge again where it sat at the base of the slopes. After waking up beside Lacey this morning and being forced to call upon every ounce of discipline he had not to roll atop her and sink inside, he'd run some errands and sought to put himself through a grueling run straight uphill to burn off his restless energy.

This thing with Lacey was nagging at him. He was starting to question if it had been wise to give in to his desire for her. She meant too much and he wanted her too much. He didn't have a sense of what she wanted from him, but he knew exactly what he wanted from her. She was the real deal for him, and he marveled at the fact he'd managed to bury his longing for so long. If it hadn't been for the geographic distance between them, he doubted he'd have managed it. Now though, he was facing the real possibility that he'd let the gates loose on his needs and wants—and she might not feel anything close to the way he felt.

To further complicate matters, the looming worry about her health amplified his feelings. His initial draw to her was bolstered by her intense strength and bravado. It was strange to see her in any way other than that, yet he felt intensely protective of her now. He had to be careful. Lacey was the single most independent woman he knew. He'd sensed this morning she needed space, so he gave it to her even though what he wanted was to wrap her in his arms and tell her to stop worrying. Of all the possible diagnoses to get, MS drove at the heart of what Lacey valued— strength and being able to conquer any situation.

While he knew quite well many people lived healthy and active lives with MS, if Lacey continued in that direction with her symptoms, he knew it would drive her batshit crazy to have to monitor herself and manage medications to prevent relapses. He wanted to rush her past the worry and fear of the unknown when he knew she wouldn't like that. Not one bit. With a shake of his head, he spun in another slow circle. The air was bracing today, autumn blowing away in the early winter winds. Snow had fallen again last night and patches of it remained where trees cast shade on the ground. He heard motion behind him and turned to see Gage running steadily up to meet him, barely appearing winded by the challenging slope.

Gage reached his side and slowed to a walk. His breath misted in the chilly air. "See you found my favorite run," Gage said by way of greeting.

Quinn grinned. "Sure did. I needed something to wear me out, and I figured running straight up the advanced slope might do it."

Gage chuckled and spun in the same circle Quinn had. "It will. I run it every day I can until it's too snowy. Can't beat the view either."

"Definitely not."

Gage circled back around to face Quinn. "I heard congratulations were in order," Gage commented. "Rumor has it you'll be the new doctor at Coastal Medical Clinic."

"Rumor has it right. I'm looking forward to it. Diamond Creek's always been one of my favorite places in Alaska."

Gage nodded. Quinn sensed Gage had something on his mind, but he didn't know Gage well enough to guess at it. Gage stared out toward the bay. "Marley had lunch with Lacey today."

Uncertain where this point was meant to go, Quinn merely nodded.

Gage looked away from the bay and over to him. "Marley'll probably let you know herself, but thanks for helping Lacey with what happened in Katmai and yesterday. I'm guessing you know damn well Lacey's not one to ask for help too often."

Quinn smiled ruefully, his heart squeezing to consider what it meant that she had actually asked him for help. "Don't I know it. She didn't really ask for help in Katmai, but she put up with it. I'm damn relieved she finally filled Marley in."

"Right. They're close, but Lacey's the tough one. You might want to be prepared for Marley to grill you about what's going on. She's worried Lacey might not tell her everything."

Quinn sighed and leaned his head back to stare at the sky before looking back to Gage. "I'm not sure how much more I can offer. The 'might have' MS part is true. No decent doctor should diagnosis it this early. It might be an isolated episode. We won't know until some time passes where she doesn't have any symptoms. I'd be glad to talk to Marley, but my guess is she's going to worry no matter what. Just like Lacey."

Gage laughed softly. "True. Anyway, I'm glad you happened to be with her. If you hadn't been, I'm not so sure she'd have bothered to see a doctor."

Quinn chuckled. "Probably not."

Gage was quiet for another few beats before he glanced to Quinn, a gleam in his eyes. "Race you down."

Quinn flicked his eyes from Gage and down the slope. "You're on!"

At that, they took off, both zigzagging their way down to the lodge. They arrived at the bottom almost in tandem. Gage slowed and circled in front of the sprawling deck behind the lodge. "Think we'll have to call it a tie. You ski much?" he asked between heaves of breath.

"Absolutely! Can't wait for the snow to fly and put some time in on the slopes here."

Gage flashed a grin just as someone called his name. Quinn glanced in the direction of the voice to see Don Peters, an older man whom Gage had introduced as his right-hand man for the lodge. Quinn had met him the other night. He lifted a hand in a wave as Gage turned to him.

"Gotta go. Maybe we'll see you at dinner tonight?"

Quinn nodded. "I'll plan on it. Catch you later."

* * *

LACEY SHOOK her head and laughed when Garrett played a card with flourish. Sitting beside Lacey, Delia rolled her eyes. "He's like a little kid when it comes to playing cards."

Cam, the ski instructor at the lodge who had recently swept Ginger off her feet, glanced over from the table he shared with Garrett and Gage. "Only when he's playing with Gage. He behaves like a normal person otherwise," Cam offered with a grin.

They were in the midst of a slow dinner at the lodge restaurant. Ginger slipped into a chair across from Lacey. "Cam likes to act like he's above it all, but every once in a while, he's as bad as the rest of them." She looked to Lacey. "Good to see you tonight. Are you done with your trips for the winter?"

Lacey nodded. "That was my last one. I have some winter trips booked, but I'm not leading any myself."

Ginger was Marley's best childhood friend and usually sly and blunt. She didn't have that edge at the moment, which made Lacey wonder if Marley had mentioned any of their conversation to her. Lacey hadn't asked Marley to keep it to herself. While she knew Marley would have respected her privacy, their social circle was too small to keep much hidden for long. Ginger brushed her shiny brown hair behind her shoulders and leaned forward to pour some wine. "Well, that's a relief. I don't know how you did it to begin with. I love the outdoors, but it's plain miserable to try to sleep outside in the winter."

Lacey heard Quinn's low chuckle beside her and couldn't help the shiver that raced through her. Another casual evening with him nearby was stirring her up inside. It was almost ridiculous the way she buzzed to life inside with him anywhere in the vicinity. Every time she looked his way, it was as if the air around them was infused with electricity.

Ginger's eyes flicked from Lacey to Quinn. "Laugh all you want. I spent one night winter camping and that was enough."

Quinn's grin flashed. "It's not so bad if you have the right gear. But, I'll be the first to agree that a long day outside in the winter is best if you're in front of a fire inside at the end of it."

Conversation carried on around Lacey with Ginger grilling Quinn about taking the job in Diamond Creek. Lacey relaxed into her chair and laughed with Delia when Garrett triumphantly won the latest card game. Her eyes kept traveling to Quinn again and again, prompting Delia to comment under her breath.

"I don't know if you wanted everyone to notice you've totally got the hots for Quinn, but you might want to try not to be so obvious if you didn't," Delia said with a soft laugh.

Lacey glanced away from Quinn to Delia on her other side, feeling her cheeks heat. She finally shrugged. She might be slightly embarrassed, but she wasn't so sure she could hide her attraction and didn't know if she wanted to try.

Delia arched a brow and smiled slowly. "Well then."

Before Lacey could say anything further, they were interrupted by Garrett who came to Delia's side and glanced down. "We've gotta go pick Nick up from basketball practice."

Delia glanced at her watch and stood up quickly. "Oh right! Let's go." She squeezed Lacey's shoulder. "I expect an update soon," she said with a sly grin.

With their departure, the group gradually filtered apart until only Lacey and Quinn were left at the table. It wasn't particularly late, and the lodge restaurant was still close to full. With the clink of silverware and glasses in the background, Lacey's awareness of Quinn notched higher. Unlike the other evening, she wasn't sandwiched against his side in the booth since they were seated at a table. Yet, the small distance between them somehow increased her body's hyper-awareness of him. She physically yearned to be closer, the sensation so acute she had to consciously keep her hand from reaching over to touch him where he sat beside her.

In the midst of her mental and emotional struggle with what was going on with her, her once steady control had deserted her. While a part of her worried about just what she was doing with Quinn, much of her welcomed the tempestuous distraction he offered. She felt so alive when he was near, practically vibrating with need and grounded in the depth of her physical attraction to him. *Maybe so, but you might be putting your heart on the line.* That was the tiny voice inside that kept occasionally pointing out how she was flirting with disaster with Quinn. She kept swatting the voice into silence, just as she did now. She recalled Marley's comment that she thought Quinn had a thing for Lacey for years. She didn't really know what a "thing" meant, but she knew she was curious. She also recalled Marley's more somber point that Lacey should try to talk to Quinn about what he wanted. That wasn't something she was quite ready to do. At the moment, she wanted nothing more than to dive into the passion shimmering around them.

She glanced to him. He was staring out the windows into the night. The moon was high above the mountains and bay tonight, not quite full, but casting a silvery glimmer across the water. He turned, his amber gaze colliding with hers. The dark desire she saw there sent the slow burn into her belly into a flash-fire. She opened her mouth to speak, but when her words failed her, she stood and grabbed his hand. He didn't hesitate, rising quickly at her side. She started to turn away, practically dragging him behind her. When she encountered resistance, she glanced back.

He looked from the table, scattered with glasses and plates, to her. "Do we need to clean up? Or, I don't know, pay the bill?" he asked with a grin.

"I have a monthly tab here, so don't worry about that. As for clean up…" She paused and scanned the restaurant, looking for Harry Lawson. Second in command to Delia in the lodge restaurant, Harry ran the restaurant dining area while Delia managed the kitchen and everything else. Harry caught her eyes from across the restaurant. In seconds he was at her side. Tall, thin and dark, Harry moved with deceptive quickness, spinning through the restaurant at all hours to take care of whatever was needed.

"Yes?" he asked.

"We were just leaving, and there's that," Lacey explained, gesturing to the table.

Harry grinned, his dark eyes flashing. "Not to worry. We'll take care of it. See you soon," he said with a wave.

At that, Lacey tightened her grip on Quinn's hand and practically ran outside. He strode alongside her once they reached the deck. A soft snow started to fall as they walked quietly toward the trees flanking the ski slope where the path wound its way to her cabin. She was burning up inside. The biting cold air only served to fan the flames within by its contrast. Quinn's hand was warm and strong around hers.

Once they were in the trees, Lacey paused and turned to him. In the shadowed light of the forest with moonlight falling through the trees and casting an otherworldly glow over them, she reached for his other hand and pulled him close. He looked down, the strong lines of his face cast in relief in the light from the moon. She leaned up, desperate to feel his lips against hers again, and he met her halfway. In flash, he fit his mouth over hers, claiming her lips in a fierce, possessive kiss. Their tongues tangled while he slid a hand down her back, his touch leaving a path of fire in its wake. His palm cupped her bottom and pulled her against him. She gasped at the feel of his hard arousal against her. Their kiss went from hot to burning, a clash of lips and teeth. By the time he pulled away and threw his head back to gulp in air, she was steaming inside and out.

Their breath misted the air around them. Lacey let her forehead fall to his chest as she tried to catch her breath. As she stood there, trying to marshal her senses, she shivered, realizing she'd completely forgotten her jacket at the lodge. She glanced up at Quinn. "I forgot my coat."

"I noticed," he said, the corner of his mouth curling in a half-smile. "Come on, let's get somewhere warm."

Without his touch leaving her, he spun her sideways, his palm a warm brand on her low back as he nudged her forward. They walked swiftly through the trees and broke into a run when they reached the small field beside her cabin. They stumbled through the door. He kicked it shut behind them and whirled her around, dipping his head and catching her lips in another fierce kiss. By the time he tore his lips free, she was almost boneless. If the door hadn't been holding her up, she'd have fallen. Heat suffused her, need pounding like a drum with every beat of her heart.

Quinn's amber eyes stared down at her, his gaze dark and intent. His shoulders rose and fell with a deep breath. He brushed her hair, damp and cool from the chilly walk back through the falling snow, away from her face before stepping back.

"Fire," he said as he toed off his boots and immediately strode to the woodstove.

For a second, she'd thought he was speaking of the burning desire between them, snapping and crackling with its own force. She almost laughed aloud when she realized he was speaking quite literally. In record time, an actual fire was brightening the dim room. Lacey kicked off her shoes and stepped toward Quinn as he closed the door to the woodstove. The flames flickered behind the glass, reflecting how she felt inside. She glanced up at him. In one step, he reached for her, picking up right where they left off moments ago.

She didn't know how many more of his kisses she could survive. She was drenched with need and frantic to feel all of him. She shoved his shirt up, which he helpfully tugged off and tossed aside. Impatient, she tore his jeans open and slipped her hand inside, a moan escaping as she felt the hard, hot length of him through his briefs. He was just as impatient as she was, swatting her hands away while he made quick work of the buttons on her shirt and tossed it aside. His eyes gleamed as he looked down. She wore a black lace bra, her nipples tight against the lace. His hands kept moving as he pushed her jeans down over her hips. She felt reckless and disordered inside, the only thing anchoring her to the moment the feel of his warm skin under her hands. Greedy to feel him, she traced a palm up over his chest, which was practically carved from stone. He mumbled something as she kicked her jeans free and turned her swiftly, sitting down on the couch with her standing between his knees.

Everything went from fast to slow with his hands stroking reverently up her legs, over the curve of her hips, into the dip of her waist, and to trace the underside of her breasts through the lace. Her breath caught when she glanced down and saw the look in his eyes. Her heart gave a hard kick, sending her pulse up another notch. He leaned forward and drew a nipple into his mouth, drenching the lace covering it. A low cry broke from her throat as he moved to the other nipple. She stroked her hands through his hair and held on, tremors running through her body.

With a flick of his thumb between her breasts, her bra fell open. He proceeded to drive her mad with need as he mapped her breasts with his lips and tongue. He paused and glanced up. She loosened her grip on his hair and shook her shoulders, letting her bra tumble to the floor. His eyes on her, he curled his hands around her hips and lifted her. Before she knew it, she was stretched out on the couch and he was sliding his palms up her calves, the calloused surface sending sparks along the surface of her skin. Her breath came in short pants as he reached the juncture of her thighs. He stroked a finger over the silk there, back and forth, back and forth. Her legs shifted restlessly, and she managed to drag her eyes open and glance down. His eyes locked to hers as he hooked a finger on the edge of her panties and dragged them over her hips roughly. She kicked them free and reached for him, only to have him shake his head sharply and grip her hips with one hand, holding her firmly in place.

"Oh no. We won't be rushing." His words were low and gruff and sent another ripple of need through her.

Without another word, he dragged his fingers through her slick folds. Her hips arched into his touch, and her breath broke on a moan when he slid one finger into her channel and then another. She lost herself in the rhythmic stroke of his fingers inside of her. She almost came the moment he brought his mouth against her, swirling his tongue around her clit. In seconds, she was crying out, her channel convulsing around his fingers. He slowed his touch and pulled away. She dragged her eyes open at the rustle of clothing to see him kicking his jeans free and rolling a condom on.

At the sight of him with the firelight flickering on his amber skin, illuminating every inch of his muscled form, her breath caught and desire tightened inside her again. He rested on one knee, his eyes mapping her body. It was as if he touched her with his gaze, lighting tiny fires on her skin. Heat suffused her and the air around them was heavy with desire. He moved slowly and deliberately, easing his weight on top of her. His elbows bracketed her face. His cock rested at her entrance, and he nudged his hips just barely, a maddening tease. On the heels of her shattering orgasm, he proceeded to stir the coals inside. His lips traveled in a blazing path down her neck, teasing her every inch of the way by nudging his cock against her entrance. Liquid need drenched the inside of her thighs as she arched into him, frantic for more.

"Quinn...I need..."

He answered with his body. With a swift surge, he seated himself deeply within her just as he closed his mouth over her nipple and bit down softly. At her ragged cry, he lifted his head.

"This?"

Somehow she managed to open her eyes to find his waiting. Wordless, she nodded and flexed into him as he began to stroke into her in long, deep surges. With his eyes on her, she held on through the building storm. She couldn't tear her eyes away, the sense of connection so deep it struck her at her core. With each stroke, she rose to meet him as he pounded harder and harder into her. Chasing bliss, she raced after it until sensation tightened in her center and spun loose, sending pleasure spiraling through her.

* * *

LACEY'S HELD FELL BACK when she cried out, the clutching heat of her channel gripping him. Quinn had been barely holding on. He finally let go, driving deeply once more before his own release crashed through him with such force, his body tightened like a bow and he collapsed against her. He eased his weight to the side and rested against her. After several moments, he felt her roll her head and opened his eyes to find her luminous green gaze on him. He reached over to brush her tangled hair out of her eyes. After several quiet moments, she bit her lip.

"Well, I guess we went a little crazy there," she said with a wondering laugh.

"That's one way to put it."

Her eyes coasted over him. He could practically see the wheels turning in her brain and wondered what she was thinking. She surprised him by reaching over and smoothing his brows. A small gesture, but oddly intimate. "We should sleep down here in front of the fire," she said softly.

He glanced around and back to her. "Works for me, but don't you think we might be a little crowded on the couch?"

She giggled. "It folds out. Let's get up and pull it out." She wiggled her hips against him. His body reacted instantly, and her eyes widened before she giggled again. He rolled his eyes and slowly lifted his weight away from her.

Not much later, Lacey had quickly tossed sheets and a quilt on the couch bed, while she directed him to make hot chocolate. She piled the bed high with pillows and grabbed the remote. "It's not that late, so let's do a movie."

Quinn handed her a mug of hot chocolate and set his own on the small table beside the couch. He crawled into the bed beside her and leaned back against the pillows. "Sounds good. You pick."

"You always say that! How come you never want to pick what we watch?" she said with a soft laugh.

He shrugged. "Because I don't care all that much."

"If it was just you, what would you watch?"

"Hmm. Probably something funny or an action flick."

She grinned and leaned back, tossing him the remote. Much later, he lay beside her, listening to the sound of her breathing. Another mind-blowing encounter with her tonight. While perhaps that should have made him worry, it was the comfort of having her curl up against him while she sipped hot chocolate that clenched his heart and made him want so much more.

<h1 style="text-align:center">CHAPTER 11</h1>

The feel of a palm sliding over the curve of her hip nudged Lacey into consciousness. She was curled on her side with Quinn spooned behind her. His hand came to rest at the dip of her waist. It felt so good to awake in the dark like this with him that she didn't dare move for fear she'd snap the sleepy, intimate moment. Once he became still again, his breathing settled into a slow, steady rhythm. She opened her eyes to find the room shrouded in darkness and the banked coals in the woodstove glimmering. It was toasty warm, although with the fire dying down, the room was cooling. She had her own personal heater curled around her. Quinn fairly simmered with warmth. She burrowed her hips closer into the cradle of his and took a deep breath, letting it out slowly.

The way she felt with him was so unlike anything she'd ever felt before, it rattled her. Yet, she couldn't turn away from it. A small voice inside of her wanted to kick off the covers and crawl out of bed, anything to tear herself free of this need to savor the intimacy between them. The rest of her shouted down that voice. She took another breath to steady herself and looked out the windows. The soft snow that had been falling when they walked to her cabin last night had stopped and the stars were twinkling bright against the sky. Her eyes fell closed and she drifted back into sleep, warm and more comfortable than she might ever have been.

A few hours later when she opened her eyes, Quinn was still curled behind her, but she sensed he was awake. She rolled over to face him. His amber gaze caught hers, and he lifted a hand to brush her hair out of her eyes.

"Mornin'."

His voice was gravelly with sleep and sent subtle wash of heat through her. It was beyond her comprehension how little he had to do to turn her on. "Good morning to you. How long have you been awake?" she asked.

"Maybe five minutes."

"Oh."

She ran out of words with that when he shifted his legs against hers, sending a jolt of heat straight to her center. His mouth curled at the corners in one of his dangerously sexy grins. Her cheeks heated, despite her best efforts to wrangle her body's response under her control. She felt as if he could see right through her. In the quiet, her phone beeped from where she'd left it on the small table behind the couch. She reached up and blindly fumbled for it, relieved for the interruption.

When she glanced at the screen, her stomach knotted. Dr. Marshall's name blinked at her. She was probably calling to confirm Lacey's MRI appointment, which was the absolute last thing Lacey wanted to think about just now. She clicked to turn the ringer off, but not before she noticed Quinn had seen the screen. She slipped her phone back onto the table. "I'll call her later," she said before kicking the covers off her legs and rolling away from Quinn.

The ice-cold dash of reality intruding snapped her out of

the warmth of the moment with Quinn. Restless and not thinking, she stood before she considered the fact she was bare naked. "I'll make pancakes, and you make coffee," she announced as she spun to face him with her hands on her hips.

His eyes darkened, and he arched a brow. "Okay," he replied, his voice gruff.

Heat slid through her veins when she saw the desire in his gaze. She suddenly became aware of her state and crossed her arms, which was somewhat pointless as her breasts only plumped over them. She whirled away and jogged up the stairs. "Be back down after I shower," she called out.

Moments later with steaming hot water sliding over her skin, she heard the shower curtain rustle and felt Quinn's hands slip around her waist. Pure carnal need flooded her as he brushed her wet hair off her neck and blazed a trail of kisses through the water. His hands came around to cup her breasts. He traced slippery circles around her nipples and tugged lightly on them. Her weak resistance, entirely of her own making, crumpled. She wanted to think she could control her response to him, but she didn't even care to try.

She spun around and placed a palm on his chest, pushing him against the tiled wall. She stroked her hands over his chest, savoring the slip and slide of the water over his sculpted muscles. Curling a fist around his cock, she bit her lip at the sound of his breath hissing through his teeth. She knelt down and licked along the underside of his cock. Her name came out on a rough gasp.

"Hmm?" she murmured as she drew him into her mouth.

She glanced up through her damp eyelashes to see his head thrown back against the shower wall, the veins in his neck standing out as she explored him with her lips and tongue. Again and again, she drew him into her mouth, sliding her fist up and down when she pulled back. She tasted a hint of salt before he yanked her up and spun her around. He suddenly froze, and she glanced over her shoulder.

His expression was pained. "Hold that thought. Have to get a condom," he bit out.

For a second, she didn't say anything and then she didn't care. She wanted to feel him, all of him, with no barriers. "No need. I'm on the pill."

His eyes slammed to hers, a question in them. "Are you sure? Because…"

"I'm sure. I trust you, so I hope you can trust me too."

His gaze darkened. "No question," he said, grabbing her hips roughly.

She had to catch her balance with her palms on the wall when her knees almost gave out as he slid his fingers between her thighs, stroking into her drenched channel. She was so ready, she could hardly bear to wait. He didn't seem inclined to make her when he positioned his cock at her entrance and surged in swiftly, seating himself all the way inside of her. Her channel throbbed around him, and she cried out at the delicious stretch of him filling her.

With Quinn's hand gripping her hip and anchoring her, she tumbled into the maelstrom of sensation overtaking her. She arched her back, her hips driving to meet each thrust of his. Abandoning herself to the storm rushing within, pleasure whipped through her. He stroked his hand around her hip and circled his thumb over her clit. The pressure inside unraveled, letting loose in a rush. Dimly, over the sound of running water and her own sharp cry, she heard a low growl from him when he drove deeply into her and felt his body tighten before his palm slapped against the wall beside one of hers.

Tremors rippled through her body as she slowly became aware of the cool tile under her palms. Quinn eased his grip on her hips and slowly pulled out, his palms sliding up her sides as she straightened. Dazed and almost boneless in the aftermath of yet another interlude with him that stole her senses and chipped away at the defenses around her heart, she slowly turned in his arms. He looked down at her for a long moment before dipping his head and catching her lips in a quick kiss. He seemed to sense she wasn't up for actually talking. His unnerving ability to read her so well was as comforting as it was disconcerting.

QUINN GLANCED AROUND HIS SUITE, his eyes scanning the perfectly made bed and otherwise almost undisturbed room. He wondered if it might make sense to call off the fiction of staying here and just cart his bag over to Lacey's cabin. The only reason he hadn't suggested it yet was he wasn't sure how Lacey would respond. He quickly changed his clothes and grabbed his lightweight down jacket off the hook by the door. The dusting of snow from last night had remained this morning under an overcast sky. He headed out of his room and downstairs, planning to swing by Dr. Daniels office to drop off some paperwork.

When he reached the foot of the stairs, he found Marley waiting by the reception desk with her baby seated in backpack on her shoulders. She was in the middle of a conversation with Harry, gesturing with her hands for emphasis. She glanced Quinn's way and waved him over.

"Well, hey there! What are you up to today?" she asked with a warm smile and a glint of curiosity in her eyes.

"A trip to town to drop some paperwork off at Dr. Daniel's office."

Marley nodded and paused to free a lock of her hair from where it was clutched in Holly's fist.

"Morning, Quinn. Hope you're enjoying your stay here," Harry said with a sly grin.

Quinn couldn't say he knew Harry well, but it was obvious Harry kept his finger on the pulse of all comings and goings from the lodge. Quinn didn't doubt for a second that Harry was quite aware Quinn hadn't spent a single night here yet. He elected not to take the bait and nodded. "I'm just happy to be in Diamond Creek," he replied, figuring he was hewing to the truth with that.

Harry's grin expanded, but he simply nodded before turning to Marley. "I need to get to the kitchen. Anything else you need?"

"Nope. Thanks for checking on that order for me."

At that, Harry pushed through a door behind the reception desk. Marley turned her gaze to Quinn, her green eyes so similar to Lacey's. She cocked her head to the side. "You're welcome to stay here, but why don't you drop the charade and take your bags over to Lacey's?" she asked, softening her blunt question with a grin.

He couldn't help but laugh. He leaned an elbow on the desk and looked over at Marley. While he wasn't so sure how Lacey would feel about him talking to Marley, he could use some feedback. "Funny you mention that because I was just thinking the same thing. I'm not so sure how Lacey would feel about that though. If you don't mind, I'll keep using the room here. If it's a problem though, say the word and..."

"It's not a problem, not at all. As for what Lacey might think, well maybe you should ask her."

"That simple, huh?"

Marley smiled ruefully. "Not simple at all. I just..." She stopped as if considering her words. "Look, maybe this is none of my business, but here goes. I think you and Lacey have a shot at something real, but she's not going to make it easy for you. You don't have to tell me if I'm right, but I think you might have had a thing for her for years." She paused, her eyes scanning his face.

He considered ignoring her point, but there wasn't much to gain by that. He nodded, swallowing against the feeling welling inside. Life, time, and geographic distance had been the factors that helped him keep his initial attraction to Lacey at bay. Problem was, it was never just an attraction. She was strong, warm, funny, kind, and independent as hell, and he loved every facet of her. The moment the word 'love' strolled through his thoughts, he almost recoiled. He was in way too deep and losing control in a way he never had. He mentally shook himself and looked at Marley again. "You'd be right," he finally said.

Her eyes lit up and then sobered quickly. "Lacey always figured she'd be on her own. I can't speak for her, but I can tell you she's pretty stirred up by all this. It may seem way too simple, but maybe if you just try to talk to her, tell her how you feel, maybe it will help."

He ran a hand through his hair and idly traced the edge of the counter with his fingertip. "We're reaching a point where one of us has to say something, so it might as well be me. Problem is, with everything else going on, I'm not so sure about the timing," he said in reference to Lacey's pending MRI and the undercurrent of tension he sensed from her.

Lacey was generally an easy-going person who thrived on taking life as it came. Yet, that was within the context of flying at life with no holds barred. Planning around potential medical concerns had never been part of the equation for her. Quinn sensed she was feeling more vulnerable than usual. He wanted more than anything to comfort her, but her tendency to push against the need for something like that was heightened.

Marley chewed on her lip and sighed. "I know, but honestly, maybe the timing is just right."

CHAPTER 12

*L*acey lay still on the narrow table, shivering slightly in the thin cotton hospital gown, while the medical technician looked down at her, peering through the fittings around Lacey's face.

"Ready?" the woman asked, her brown eyes warm.

Lacey nodded, her eyes landing on the woman's name tag as the woman straightened. 'Suzanne, MRI Technician' was all the tag offered. Lacey heard the sound of a button and then the machine started to move as she slid inside a circular tube. She closed her eyes and tried to calm her insides. This was just a scan. Dr. Marshall would review the results and let her know. It didn't have to be the giant thing it had become in her brain. Ever since she'd called Dr. Marshall back, her brain had ping-ponged between worrying about this stupid scan and obsessing about Quinn. Whenever she wearied of one subject, she bounced to the other. With Quinn, she worried over how to manage the intensity of her feelings for him. The strange thing about Quinn was that when she was with him in the immediacy of the moment, her worries went up in smoke.

She hadn't told anyone when she scheduled this, thinking she needed to face her fears on her own. Right now though, with the odd metallic clanging of the MRI echoing around her, she felt cold and alone and wished Quinn was waiting outside for her. They'd fallen into a pattern of nights that were nothing more than a blur of sensation and days where they went their separate ways after a leisurely breakfast. They'd yet to talk, although Marley had nudged her about it again. She didn't know what to do with her feelings and every time they started to overwhelm her, her mind spun in another direction as she contemplated how she might have to adjust her life if it turned out she had MS. She started to shake her head and remembered she needed to try to lie still. With a sigh, she squeezed her hands together where they were clasped on her chest.

She didn't know how long the MRI took, but she was relieved when the echoing clicks stopped. A while later, she dressed in the sterile dressing room and exited out into the hallway at the hospital. Dr. Marshall had assured her she would call once she reviewed the results, so Lacey figured she didn't need to hang around. She'd gotten chilly in the thin hospital gown and couldn't seem to shake it even though she bundled up in a lightweight down jacket. She stopped in front of the revolving door at the hospital entrance and looked out through the windows. Snow had started to fall during her appointment, obscuring the mountains across the bay. The sky was overcast and the bay slate gray, matching her internal state. She took a deep breath and glanced down to zip her jacket, only to jump when she heard her name, a smile spreading inside and out at the sound of Quinn's voice.

When she glanced up, he was walking toward her from another hallway in the hospital. "Came to find you, but I think I went the wrong way," he said with a grin.

She shrugged, warmth curling around her heart and easing the tension inside. "They don't make it easy. You'd think the signs might help, but they're a little vague."

He reached her and slid his palms down her arms to wrap around her hands. His grip was strong and warm, steadying her even further. "You could've mentioned you were coming here today. I'd have been on time then," he said, his grin turning rueful.

She shrugged, trying to tamp down how pleased she was that he searched her out. She wanted to curl up into him and forget her worries about her health. "I should've said something, but you found me anyway. I don't have any news though. Dr. Marshall said she'd call as soon as she reviews the results."

"I knew you wouldn't have the results yet, but it's not fun to come to places like this alone. That's all," he said, his voice low and his eyes intent on her.

Her throat tightened and she managed a nod. "It's not." She squeezed his hands and looked out the window again. "It looks like we might have our first winter storm tonight. Pizza and movies?"

"Sounds like a plan."

He freed one of her hands and turned to walk outside with her.

THE FOLLOWING MORNING, Quinn slung his backpack over his shoulder as he stepped outside. Lacey's prediction about the first winter storm had proven to be true with a foot of snow falling during the night. It was only November though, so the morning's bright sun had already melted several inches of it. Light glistened where the snow melted. He strode to his SUV and tossed his backpack in the back. Before climbing in, he scanned the view beyond the lodge.

The snow-capped peaks across the bay were stark against the blue sky. After yet another night with Lacey where Quinn meant to try to broach a conversation about what was happening between them, he hadn't been able to bring himself to break the spell. She'd seemed out of sorts after the MRI. By the time she seemed to settle back to herself, they were lounging on the couch with her legs thrown over his lap, and he couldn't bring himself to ruin the moment by trying to talk about something he knew was likely to get her guard up.

This morning, he was on his way back to Willow Brook to empty the storage unit he'd kept there while he was overseas. He hoped to check in on his mother and see that she was settled back at home, along with another visit with his sister. When he'd left Lacey's this morning, he'd experienced something he'd never experienced—a sense of what he'd miss while he was away. Marley had rolled her eyes this morning when she saw him in the hallway. She'd adjusted Holly in her arms and paused at his side. "Have you tried to talk to Lacey yet?" she asked, not even bothering with a greeting. When he quickly shook his head, she continued. "You two are clearly meant for each other, but I can't get you to talk to each other."

At Quinn's abashed shrug, Marley smiled and tugged him into a quick hug. "You're welcome to stay here again if you need to when you're back. How long will it be before you're back anyway?"

"A few weeks. I've got some things to deal with up there. After that, I'm here for good. Thanks for the offer."

Staring out over the bay, watching wispy clouds drift across the sky, he wished he knew how to handle this situation with Lacey. While he had some clarity about how he felt for her, he had no experience with serious relationships. His life hadn't allowed the opportunity. Between college, backcountry guiding and then medical school, there hadn't been room for commitment. Even though he'd taken one look at Lacey the moment he met her and felt his body hum with need, he hadn't spent much time dwelling on her. Mostly because she hadn't shown the slightest return of any affection beyond friendship. In a short span of time, that had spun sideways. Between trying to adjust to it and trying to fumble his way through without potentially blowing up their friendship, he didn't quite know how to talk about it with her. While he respected Marley's point that they needed to talk, it would help if he knew where to start.

All of this was complicated with Lacey's reaction to her potential medical diagnosis. In some ways, he wished for clarity on that front soon because at least then she would know what she was facing, as would he. Without her saying a word about it, he knew she was torn with the uncertainty and wishing upon wish it would all pass. If it wasn't going to pass, knowing Lacey the way he did, he figured she'd be able to accept it the sooner she knew. Occasionally, disquieting thoughts danced along the edges of his mind—wondering how Lacey might change if she had MS, not in the physical sense, but in who she was, and what that might mean for them.

Quinn took a last look around before climbing into his car and driving away. As he crested the hill that dipped down into Diamond Creek, he glanced in his rear view mirror, savoring the last glimpse of the place he was about to make his home.

* * *

LACEY STOOD on the rocky shore and looked out over the water. A cold wind blew sideways, ruffling the surface. A few seagulls swooped through the air, calling to each other above the wind. She took a slow breath, enjoying the rush of energy that came from the chilled air and the salty scent of the ocean mingled with a hint of spruce. She'd come to another beach for a run today. She'd promised herself she wouldn't run too far this time. This beach, like every inch of the coastline here, offered a glorious view of Kachemak Bay, yet it was within sight of Diamond Creek. The spruce forest thinned as it approached the ocean, and a small clearing provided parking nearby instead of down along a path like her old favorite, Raven's Beach.

Dr. Marshall had assured her she could keep running, but advised she be alert to how she felt. Lacey chafed at the suggestion, but she wasn't stupid and didn't want to end up too far away to access help if she needed it. After Quinn left for Willow Brook yesterday, she'd missed him so acutely, she was determined to run today. She needed something to clear her mind.

She mentally scanned her body and set off at a slow jog. She allowed herself to pick up to a fairly brisk run, but held back from pushing herself to the point of exhaustion. After an hour, she slowed to a jog and then a walk as she approached the parking area. She was almost giddy to have managed a solid hour of running without experiencing any weakness and tingling in her legs. Maybe this 'episode' was over and she'd never have another. Her mood high, she climbed into her car and drove back to her cabin. She needed a shower, but then she planned to round up Marley for a coffee date. Somehow, she hadn't been to Misty Mountain Café since she'd been home and she needed to remedy that today.

A few hours later, Lacey had a coffee from Misty Mountain in hand, but Marley wasn't with her and she was fighting back tears. After a quick lunch with Marley who had to race back to the lodge after she got a call from Gage that the computer server at the lodge had crashed, Lacey had swung by Dr. Marshall's office. Dr. Marshall had left a brief message to check in about the MRI results, so Lacey figured now as good a time as any to meet with her. The high from her run had left Lacey feeling like she was back to her familiar health and strength. Somehow, in the span of a few short hours, she convinced herself this was nothing more than a surreal blip in her health.

Wishful thinking and confidence were turning out to be nothing more than a mirage. Dr. Marshall sat in front of her, quietly talking through something, while Lacey tried to get a handle on herself. Dr. Marshall had started off by saying the MRI had confirmed two areas of nerve damage. Lacey barely heard what she said next. Even though Quinn had cautioned her against it, Lacey had done some online sleuthing about MS, so she'd know what to look for. She didn't claim to be a doctor, but one detail that stood out in neon in her mind was a diagnosis of MS required two areas of nerve damage and ruling out all other possible diagnoses.

"Lacey, are you with me?"

Lacey mentally shook herself and looked up at Dr. Marshall. "Um, I lost track there." She held onto her coffee cup for dear life, its warmth anchoring her and keeping her from dissolving into tears of despair.

Dr. Marshall set her computer tablet on the counter and swiveled her chair to face Lacey directly where she sat on a hard plastic chair in the exam room. Dr. Marshall adjusted her glasses on her nose and angled her head to the side. Her short dark brown hair was streaked with gray, and she had a regal look to her with her angular features and intelligent eyes.

"I don't know where your thoughts are running off to, but let's slow down."

Lacey nodded and swallowed against the tightness in her throat. She was annoyed with herself for being so silly today and getting all excited. She should've known she needed to wait for the MRI results.

"The MRI shows nerve damage in two small areas. This

still doesn't mean with certainty that you have MS," Dr. Marshall said softly. She watched Lacey for another moment, her eyes sharp and assessing. "I've known you since you were a little girl, Lacey. You've always been so much fun because you literally ran at life and hugged it with both arms. I can only imagine how it feels for you to hear you might have any kind of medical condition, much less one that could slow you down a little bit. Even if you are officially diagnosed with MS, all signs so far point to the likelihood you have the relapsing-remitting type. You *will* be able to live the life you want with a few adjustments."

Lacey was barely able to tolerate the comfort in Dr. Marshall's voice and honed in on one detail. "What do you mean 'if'? You just said I had two areas of nerve damage. Isn't that what you need to make a diagnosis?"

Dr. Marshall narrowed her eyes. "I specifically asked Quinn not to go into the medical details with you."

Lacey shook her head. "He didn't! I mean, I asked him some questions after my visit to the hospital in Anchorage, but he hasn't said anything else new and kept telling me to wait to talk with you about the results. If you're wondering why I thought that, it's because I looked online. Quinn told me it wasn't a good idea, but I had to know what to keep an eye out for. Just tell me what it all means," she said with a sigh.

Dr. Marshall's gaze softened. "Okay then. It's true that we need to confirm two areas of nerve damage, which we've done. Truthfully, adding everything together, it certainly looks like you have MS. But first, I need to run a few more tests to rule out other possibilities. Fortunately, I've been your doctor for years, so we have all your medical records, which are pretty damn boring overall, but a good resource for comparison." She swiveled in her chair and picked up her computer tablet again. "Let me order those tests and then..."

"If you're pretty sure, can't we just say it is what it is?" Lacey heard the slightly whiny tone to her voice and flinched. She hated, absolutely hated, this uncertainty. It gnawed at her and made her feel shaky inside.

Dr. Marshall tapped the screen of her tablet and set it back on the counter. "I'm willing to say it's looking like a definite possibility, but we do need to rule a few things out first. I've already ordered the tests. Stop by the lab at the hospital this afternoon." She swiveled her chair again and removed her glasses. "I know you want a firm answer, but maybe you could work on accepting that you will most likely be dealing with these symptoms in some capacity. Schedule an appointment to see me the day after tomorrow. I'll have the lab results then."

Lacey didn't like the answer, but she knew it was childish and pointless to argue when Dr. Marshall had made it very clear why she was waiting. She stood up and snagged her jacket off the back of the chair, putting it on an arm at a time because she couldn't seem to let go of her cup of coffee. As she drove home, her eyes scanned the landscape. The snow from the first storm last night had mostly melted, leaving behind damp fallen grass and leaves. The winding road up to her cabin passed by a field of fireweed, which bloomed in a blaze of fuchsia glory at the end of summer. The bright petals had faded to pink and were scattered on the ground, their faded color the only brightness in her day.

She mentally beat herself up over how poorly she was handling this whole mess. It wasn't like she had a terminal illness. In her online meandering, she knew many people with MS lived long, healthy and active lives. It was just that the very idea of a medical problem of any kind struck at the core of how she defined herself. She didn't know who she would be if she wasn't Brawny. That's what kept bothering her. Every time she thought about it, she felt confused and uncertain inside...and vulnerable, so, so vulnerable.

She reached the gravel drive leading to her cabin and turned into it. When she came to a stop and looked up at the charming little cabin with its bright red roof, a pang of longing hit her. She wished Quinn were here so much it almost hurt.

CHAPTER 13

Quinn's phone buzzed in his coat pocket, indicating a text had arrived. He was in the middle of helping his mother into a recliner. It wasn't just any recliner, but a rather elaborate recliner that slowly rotated from standing to sitting. He'd purchased it this morning once he heard from Amelia their mother had fallen already getting out of her chair.

"All you need to do is rest your hips on the edge here," Quinn paused to gesture to the chair. "Then, you push the button here on the armrest, or on the remote, and the chair will slowly move back on its own. When you need to get up, it does the opposite. Try it."

His mother rolled her eyes, but she gamely rested her hips on the edge after leaning her cane against a table beside the chair. She pushed the button and the chair eased back. When it stopped moving, she grinned up at him. "Okay, I'm sold. With this, I probably won't fall trying to get up."

Quinn stepped away and sat down in a nearby rocking chair. "Glad you like it. I set up a walk through with the woman from the rehab center. I don't know why you didn't let them do that before you moved back. She'll go through the house and make suggestions for modifications to minimize the chance you'll hurt yourself. I'm glad you're home and mobile again, but it's going to be a while before you can manage without support. I don't want you here alone unless we can at least try to make it easier on you. It's plain luck Amelia happened to stop by right after you fell."

His mother looked away from him to stare out the window. Her home in Willow Brook was situated at the edge of the forest with cottonwood and birch trees to one side and spruce on the other. The home faced a field with a view of Denali, the tallest peak in the North America, in the distance. A lake centered in the view was host to a flock of trumpeter swans every summer. His mother loved her home. He'd always known it wouldn't be easy on her when age started to catch up to her, but he hoped they could make the home more easy to navigate for now. She looked back to him, her dark brown gaze resigned.

"Fine. I thought I could be careful enough that it wouldn't matter. As happy as I am to be back home, even I have to admit I'm not getting around the way I used to. I never thought I'd be attached to that damn cane, but I'm getting there," she said with a soft laugh. Her eyes sobered. "Thank you for helping. I need to apologize to your sister. She tried to insist on the same thing before I moved home last week. I pooh-poohed it and told her she was being silly."

Quinn shrugged. "She'll appreciate your change of heart more than the apology."

His mother threw her head back with a laugh. "So true." Her laugh slowed and she glanced to him again. "How long will you be here before you move to Diamond Creek?"

"Another week or so. Dr. Daniels said he could be flexible about when I start, but I'd like to get there and settled as soon as I can. I don't like too much time on my hands, so..."

Sarah's lips quirked. "No, you never were one to twiddle your thumbs. I had a feeling this would work out, so I'm thrilled it did. How's Lacey doing?"

Sarah had met Lacey a number of times over the years when they had breaks between backcountry trips. Quinn hadn't been able to bring himself to fill her in on whatever was going on between him and Lacey, but he had shared his concerns about Lacey's medical issues.

"All in all, she's annoyed as hell, but doing okay. You know Lacey. She thrives on living on the edge. She's not too pleased to think any medical issue might get in her way."

"Can't say I blame her," Sarah said with a wry grin. "Tell her if I can accept it, she can too."

Quinn chuckled. "You got it."

Their conversation moved on to more mundane topics before Quinn waited patiently while his mother made her way into the kitchen. She was bound and determined to make dinner for him and Amelia.

Hours later as Quinn closed the door on the guest room in his mother's house, his phone buzzed again. As he was slipping it out of his pocket, he recalled he'd never checked it earlier. Lacey's name flashed on the screen for texts and a missed call. Her latest text was brief.

Never mind.

Never mind what? Quinn pulled up his messages and saw she'd left two messages hours ago. As he read them, his chest tightened with worry and annoyance with himself for completely forgetting to check his phone earlier.

Got the results from the MRI. Not looking too good.

His heart clenched and his stomach churned with worry. He wished like hell she'd called him. *Uh, dude, she texted you and you ignored it for like four hours. Hey, I didn't ignore it on purpose. I was busy and forgot to look. Okay, fine. On her end, it probably seemed like you were ignoring it.* He shook his head, frustrated with the back and forth in his mind. He scrolled down on the phone screen to see her next text, which came roughly an hour after the first.

Just tried to call. Guess you're busy. Let me know a time I could maybe call.

He glanced at the time. It was past ten, but she'd just texted him, so he knew she was awake. Without giving himself a chance to reconsider, he tapped the screen to call her.

The phone rang enough times that Quinn was about to hang up. As he pulled the phone away from his ear, he heard Lacey's hello.

"Hey!" he said as he almost slammed the phone against his ear. "Sorry I missed your texts and your call earlier. I was helping my mom, then we had dinner and then...well, you know how it goes." He paused for a breath. "Tell me what Dr. Marshall said about the MRI results," he said softly, cutting straight to the point.

Lacey sigh came through the phone, weary and strained. "She confirmed two areas of nerve damage. She still won't say it's MS because she said she has to rule out some other things first. I'm just tired of it already. I'd rather know for sure and then I know what I'm dealing with." Lacey's voice vibrated with frustration.

Quinn considered how to reply. He wished upon wish he were there with her because what he really wanted to do was pull her in his arms and hold her. He didn't think there was much he could say that would alleviate how she felt right now. Her frustration and impatience were entirely understandable, but he knew what was bothering her the most was how this struck at her view of herself. "Look, I know it's frustrating, but Dr. Marshall is right to wait." He bit back the urge to run down a list of questions about what she planned to test for rule outs because it wouldn't be productive and would likely send Lacey on an online investigation. He figured she'd ignored his suggestion to steer clear of researching on her own because that was the kind of thing she'd do.

"I'll be back by tomorrow," he said, surprising himself with his announcement. He could finish taking care of what he needed to here tomorrow morning, but he would be pushing it. Yet, all he wanted was to be back by Lacey's side. Hearing the undercurrent of anxiety in her voice prompted an almost visceral response in him.

"Really?" Lacey asked, the hopefulness in her question making it a certainty he'd be there.

"Absolutely. I've taken care of a few things for Mom. I still have to empty my stuff out of storage, but that won't take more than the morning."

"Oh good. How's your mom?"

"All in all, she's pretty good. She's home, and I've set it up for someone from the rehab center to do a walk through and make recommendations for modifications around the house."

Conversation moved onto a few other mundane matters, while Quinn shrugged out of his shirt and kicked his jeans off to climb in bed. Roughly an hour later, he found himself resting against the pillows, chuckling as Lacey shared a story of an errant salmon while dip-netting last summer. When his laugh faded, he realized he just plain didn't want to get off the phone. He felt like a schoolboy from days gone by, back when talking on the phone was the end all be all.

Lacey quieted, and he heard the soft sound of her taking a breath. "I suppose we should get off the phone, huh?"

"If we want to get any sleep, then maybe so."

She laughed softly, the sound curling around his heart. "You have a long day tomorrow if you're packing and driving all the way here."

"It won't be too bad," he said, failing to keep from yawning.

"Where are you staying?" she asked suddenly.

"Uh, haven't really figured that out yet. Marley said I could stay at the lodge until..."

"You can stay here until you find a place," she said quickly.

Startled, all he could manage was a nod. After a long silence, he realized she couldn't see him. "That'd be great. I looked into a few options for rentals, but I haven't hammered anything out yet."

After a few beats, she spoke again. "Good night. Call me when you're almost here."

"You got it. Good..."

The click of the phone in his ear cut off his words. He slowly lowered the phone and set it on the nightstand, a small smile curling his lips. He figured Lacey had just about outdone herself actually inviting him to stay with her. As he drifted off to sleep, it occurred to him he'd committed himself to an insanely busy day tomorrow—all because he couldn't bear to go any longer without seeing Lacey.

* * *

LACEY TUGGED on the heavy door to the lodge and stepped through with a gust of icy wind. She pushed her hood back. "Whew! It's hella windy out there today," she said as Harry looked up from the reception desk.

He arched a dark brow and grinned. "Definitely. You here for breakfast with the girls this morning?"

"Of course. Is Marley still upstairs?"

He shook his head and gestured through the archway into the restaurant. "She's in the back booth with Delia."

Lacey gave a little wave as she walked past him. "Thanks Harry! See you later."

As promised, Marley and Delia were seated in the back corner booth, the one permanently reserved for friends and family. It was conveniently tucked so close to the kitchen, it wouldn't have been considered a good place to sit as a paying customer. It was immediately beside the swinging door into the kitchen as well, which meant for an almost constant flow of traffic. For friends and family, it was perfect. Lacey slipped into the booth beside Marley and leaned over to kiss her on the cheek. "Hey sis! Where's Holly?"

Marley turned to her with a wide smile. "With Mom for the morning. She wanted some baby time, and I get a break."

Delia cast her warm smile between them. "A few hours baby free is awesome, but it's weird. Or it was for me when Nick was little."

Marley twirled a loose lock of hair around her finger and cocked her head to the side as if she was considering it. "I suppose it is odd. I'm so used to being with Holly all the time, it's weird." She shrugged. "But it's okay. Mom came by to pick her up first thing this morning. Showering without racing through it was pretty sweet."

Delia burst out laughing at the look on Lacey's face. "Trust me, if you ever have kids, you'll find yourself unbelievably excited about the most mundane things, like an uninterrupted shower."

Lacey giggled. "Okay, I get it. Anyway, so what else is new?"

Harry stopped by the table. "Okay ladies, do you need me to assign someone to your table, or is everyone doing the buffet this morning?"

"Buffet!" They all spoke at once.

Harry grinned. "Got it. I'll get fresh coffee for everyone."

He spun away and pushed through the swinging door into the kitchen.

They collectively rose and filled their plates at the buffet. After they were seated and Harry delivered their coffees, conversation moved on to the slow wind down of the crazy tourist season in Diamond Creek. Every summer, the population of the community effectively quadrupled with the amount of tourists flocking to the area.

Marley finished a bite of eggs and gestured with her fork. "They have to put in stop lights at those two main intersections soon. I waited over ten minutes to turn onto the highway a few weeks ago."

Delia shrugged. "Every time it's come up, too many people say it will ruin the town's character. Anyway, things don't slow down as much as they used to with the lodge back in business," she said with a satisfied smile.

"We bring plenty of business to town, but it's not quite the way it is in the summer," Marley replied.

"The lodge brings just enough people here to keep town from being too sleepy in the winter, but I wouldn't want the summer season all year. It's too crazy," Lacey added.

A customer stopped by, interrupting their conversation, and asked Marley about the hiking trails. While Marley chatted with the customer, Delia caught Lacey's eyes. "Any word on when Quinn is officially moving here?"

"He'll be here later today," Lacey said, her heart giving a little kick at the thought.

She'd managed to fall asleep last night, but it had taken a while. Between being out of sorts over her medical tests and missing Quinn like crazy, her mind had been spinning in circles.

Delia's eyes crinkled at the corners with her smile. "I guess that's a good thing, huh?"

Lacey flushed. Before she had a chance to reply, Marley finished her other conversation and turned back to them as the customer walked off. She took a sip of coffee, her eyes bouncing between them. "What?"

Lacey's cheeks got hotter. She shrugged and took a gulp of her coffee.

Delia glanced from her to Marley. "All I did was ask when Quinn would be back."

"When will he be back?" Marley asked, her eyes turning to Lacey.

"Later today," Lacey mumbled before taking a bite of scrambled eggs.

"Oh great. Did he mention if he needed to stay here? I told him he could."

Lacey swallowed and pointlessly moved her food around on her plate as she answered. "He's staying with me." Somehow saying aloud that he'd be staying with her made things feel quite real.

She could feel Delia and Marley's eyes on her. She finally gave in and looked up.

"Well, that's good then. I don't think he spent a single night at the lodge when he was here. Might as well stop tiptoeing around. Have you two actually talked yet?" Marley asked.

Delia muffled a laugh behind her hand when Lacey's mouth dropped open. Lacey swung her gaze to Delia. "What's so funny?" she asked, trying to tamp down her embarrassment.

"Just you. You've always been such a badass. I don't think you ever even noticed a guy before, not even Quinn. Now, you're so obviously head over heels with him," Delia replied.

Lacey figured her face must be practically neon red at this point. She took another gulp of coffee and tried to marshal her composure. Delia's eyes softened. "I can't help but tease, but I didn't mean to make you uncomfortable."

Lacey bit her lip and shook her head, fighting the sudden tightness in her throat and the tears threatening. After a few deep breaths, she managed to beat back her tears. She glanced between Delia and Marley who were both quiet. "I'm fine. It's just...ugh..." She paused to wipe at her eyes, the tears immediately welling again. "This is ridiculous. I'm an emotional mess, and I hate being like this."

Marley slipped her arm across Lacey's shoulders and gave her a squeeze. "Is everything okay with Quinn? I thought you were happy he was moving here."

Lacey dragged her sleeve across her eyes and nodded. "I am. I just, I don't know. I've never been like this about a guy, and I feel stupid and silly. There's that and then I saw Dr. Marshall the other day, and..." A tear escaped and rolled down her cheek.

Marley and Delia waited patiently, which made Lacey want to cry even harder. She quickly filled them in on the details from Dr. Marshall and the continued uncertainty. Delia, the calm center of their small social circle, nodded solemnly. "So, when will you see her to review the lab results?"

Lacey took a shaky breath and let it out in a sigh. "See, that's the problem. I blew off going to the lab for the follow up tests. I was tired and I just didn't want to deal with it."

"Want me to go with you tomorrow?" Marley asked, her eyes concerned.

Lacey shook her head. "I'll go. I promise. If I don't, Quinn will drag me down there anyway."

Marley smiled softly. "That's one more mark in his favor. I have no doubt he'll make sure you get your butt down to the lab." She paused, her eyes assessing. "You know, it's not so bad to be confused about this thing with Quinn, but I mean it when I say I think you two could have a real chance. Just be careful not to get in your own way."

"What do you mean?" Lacey asked quickly.

"Just that. You saw me stumble plenty before I got my head clear when it came to Gage. You're one of the strongest women I know. I'm guessing it's not exactly easy to feel the way you do about Quinn. That's all."

Lacey chewed on her lip and brushed her hair away

from her eyes, thinking it was so *not* easy that it made her half-crazy. "Maybe so. How come there aren't instructions for this kind of thing?"

Delia almost spit out her coffee at that. Her burst of laughter was infectious, lightening Lacey's mood as she realized how ridiculous her question was.

CHAPTER 14

Quinn stared into the empty storage space. With his lifestyle, he hadn't had much to store beyond extra gear for backcountry trips and some books. Every box was stacked tidily in the back of his SUV. He stood there, an odd feeling washing over him. His life for the last decade or so had been one temporary situation after another. He always circled back to Alaska, but even then nothing was settled. He was about to move to Diamond Creek and commit himself to a place and a life in a way he never had before. Lacey bolted into his thoughts, and he chuckled to himself. Even his mind conjured her just as she was—bold and strong. Lacey wasn't one who strolled anywhere. She walked with purpose.

When he'd told Amelia and his mother that he'd decided to speed up his return back to Diamond Creek, they'd glanced between each other and grinned.

"Didn't think you could hold off too much longer without getting back to Lacey," Amelia had commented with a sly smile.

"How...?"

Amelia arched a brow. "The look in your eyes whenever she comes up."

His mother had merely leaned over and kissed him on the cheek where they sat at the table in her kitchen. He shook his head now, realizing they knew him so well that they'd known precisely what lay in his heart without him having said a word about it. He turned away from the empty storage space and tugged on the cord to roll the door down. After a quick stop by the storage office to close out his rental, he climbed into his SUV for the drive to Diamond Creek. It was late afternoon, and five hours of driving were between him and Lacey.

By the time he crested the rise above Diamond Creek, he was starting to get weary from the drive. He'd watched a breathtaking sunset along the way, but darkness had fallen hours ago. He'd tracked the rise of the almost full moon above the mountains across the bay as he got closer to Diamond Creek. The town lay glittering at the bottom of the hill, the moon high in the sky, bathing the bay in a silvery glow. He let out a breath and kept driving, turning onto the road that led up toward the lodge and Lacey's cabin nearby. He quickly tapped the dash screen to call Lacey.

"Hey," she said immediately after the first ring.

"Hey to you. You said to call when I was close. I'm almost there."

"Yay! Okay, see you in a few."

He gunned his SUV and zipped up the winding hill. His pulse was pounding and anticipation was coursing through him. Moments later, he turned into the gravel drive that led through the trees to her cabin. He parked quickly and ran up the steps. Lacey flung the door open, the lights on the deck illuminating her. Her auburn hair fell in a tousle around her shoulders. She wore a pair of fleece leggings and a t-shirt that hugged her generous breasts. He closed the distance between them and lifted her into his arms. She giggled into his neck. It felt so damn good to hold her again, his heart squeezed and his throat tightened. A distant voice cautioned he needed to get a grip, but at the moment he didn't care to listen.

When she lifted her head and leaned back, her green eyes were bright. "Hey again," she said, her voice throaty.

A blast of icy wind gusted across the deck, and she shivered in his arms. He was so hot, inside and out, he barely noticed it. "Hey, let's get inside before you freeze."

Without letting her go, he stepped through the door. She didn't seem any more inclined to let go of him and wrapped her legs around his waist. His almost instant arousal when he'd seen her hardened further when he felt the heat of her against him. With a kick, he managed to close the door behind them. He spun around and put her back against the door before catching her lips in a fierce kiss. He poured his longing and pounding need into their kiss. She threaded her hands in his hair, gripping tightly as he plundered her mouth with his lips, tongue and teeth.

He lost all sense of time as their kiss went on and on. Her hands roamed down his back and around to the front before she tore at the buttons on his jeans. Plastered between him and the door, she adroitly managed to slip her hand inside his briefs and curl a hand around his cock. He tore his lips free and groaned.

"Holy hell, Lace. What you do to me..."

He growled into her neck and bit down softly, grinning with satisfaction when she gasped and threw her head back against the door.

"Hold on," he said as he stepped back and eased her down.

He was beyond the point of finesse and only wanted to be deep inside of her. In one swift move, he shoved her leggings and panties over her hips and to her ankles. She kicked them free where they spun on the floor. He knelt down before her and ran his palms up her legs. She was a pure miracle of strength and softness. His hands reached the juncture of her thighs where her auburn hair graced her. He dropped kisses on the inside of her thighs and ignored her when she threaded a hand in his hair and tugged. He had to taste her. He dragged a finger through her folds, which were drenched. Gripping her hip with one hand, he stroked into her channel with one finger and then another. She clenched around his touch and a low moan broke from her. He brought his mouth to her, swirling his tongue in a circle around the nub of her desire before exploring her folds as he kept up a slow rhythm of strokes into her channel. Her hips arched into his touch and her breath came in ragged pants. He circled his thumb over her clit before sucking it into his mouth, smiling against her when she cried out and stiffened.

* * *

LACEY WAS SHAKING, inside and out. She could hardly stand as pleasure rolled through her in waves. If she hadn't been leaning against the door, she was certain she'd have collapsed. Quinn slowly dragged his fingers out as his mouth went on a meandering exploration of her body on his way up. Her shirt was drawn up slowly as he came to standing. With a yank, he pulled it over her head and tossed it aside. Still reverberating from her climax, need kept clawing at her. She needed him inside of her. *Now.* She shoved his jeans down around his hips, freeing his cock. There. That's what she needed. She didn't have to ask because he stepped closer and lifted her against him again. Her legs reflexively curled around his hips.

With his amber eyes on her, nearly searing her with their intensity, he positioned his cock at her entrance and sheathed himself inside her in one swift motion. She closed her eyes, soaking in the delicious stretching sensation. He held still for a long moment and adjusted his hold on her, curling both hands around her hips. He whispered her name, his voice sending a prickle over her skin.

It took effort, but she managed to open her eyes. The moment his gaze locked to hers again, she couldn't have looked away if she tried. He started to move with long, deep thrusts into her. She flexed against him, straining to get closer with every stroke. From the echoes of her first climax, another built. The pressure tightened inside. The gathering storm rose to a crescendo within. With another deep surge inside of her, the storm let loose, sending sharp streaks of pleasure through her. She gripped his back and held on as her body rippled, her channel clenching around him. One more stroke, and he threw his head back with a growl, his body going taut as a bow before he shuddered against her. His head fell into the curve of her neck.

They stayed like that for several long moments. Their breath slowed in unison. She gradually became aware of the cold door against her back, a contrast to the warmth of Quinn. She stroked a hand through his hair, and he lifted his head.

"Nice to see you," he said, his voice gravelly. A corner of his mouth curled in a grin.

She bit her lip. A laugh bubbled out. "You too."

* * *

A WHILE LATER, after they'd showered together, Quinn rolled his head on the back of the couch to look at Lacey. She'd declared she had a few work things to do online, so she was busy tapping away on her laptop. His stomach growled, and she looked up.

"I bet you're starving. Should we order pizza?"

He glanced at his watch, which told him it was just past nine. "Kinda late, but I'm pretty hungry."

She grinned when his stomach announced its agreement. "Hang on. I can order online with Glacier Pizza. What kind do you want?"

"Pepperoni."

She clicked a few things on the screen. "Done! It says a half hour for delivery. They're usually quicker, so hang tight."

Later on, Quinn lay against the pillows on Lacey's bed and turned his head to look out into the night sky. The moon was sitting fat and round over the mountains and the stars glittered brightly. Lacey was curled up against him with her head tucked into his shoulder. He wondered if his heart could take it if it turned out Lacey didn't want what he did. He also wondered if his worries about blowing up their friendship were a genuine reality if he couldn't find his way through this somehow. It was becoming more and more clear that might not be possible, not with the depth of the feeling held within his heart. With a mental shake, he stroked his palm in a slow circle on her back and gradually fell asleep.

CHAPTER 15

*L*acey kicked a loose pebble across the parking lot as she walked beside Marley to the lab. Quinn had offered to go with her, as she'd guessed he would, but he got a call from Dr. Daniels right when they were discussing it, and Marley stopped by with Holly. As soon as Marley ascertained the situation, she offered to go with Lacey. Quinn had started to insist he'd take her, but Lacey didn't want him to feel like he had to hover. During a brief verbal tug-of-war, Holly latched onto Lacey's sleeve and wouldn't let go, effectively deciding the matter. Quinn had insisted she call him with any updates as he followed them outside.

She and Marley walked slowly through the revolving door into the hospital and down the hallway to the lab. The hospital in Diamond Creek could have been any hospital in the world with its neutral décor and sterile vibe. After Lacey gave her name to the receptionist in the lab, she sat beside Marley who carefully set Holly on the beige carpeted floor. Holly set to chewing on her latest favorite stuffed toy, a bright green frog with rubbery feet. Lacey didn't notice she was tapping her fingers restlessly on the sleek wooden armrest of her chair until Marley glanced her way, her eyes flicking from her tapping fingers to her face.

"So, how are things with Quinn?" Marley asked.

"He just got here last night. I don't have much of an update," Lacey replied, slightly annoyed at Marley's question, in part because she knew Marley was focusing on Quinn to distract her from the lab tests.

Marley reached down to stroke Holly's hair when Holly carefully pulled herself up onto Marley's knee. "Yeah, but how are you feeling about things?" Marley asked, undeterred by Lacey's sidestep.

Lacey sighed. "Same as before. Things feel great when we're together and every time I try to think past that, I get anxious. I'm not so sure now is the best time to have this conversation though."

Marley's eyes lit up when she smiled. "Right. Probably not. But hey, I'll take it as a bonus that you only got sort of annoyed with me."

Lacey mock-punched her in the arm and laughed softly. At that moment, the door off the side of the small waiting room opened and a woman wearing a neon green hospital shirt smiled broadly. "Lacey?"

"That's me," Lacey replied, standing up quickly.

"I'm Violet," the woman said, holding a hand out.

Lacey shook it quickly and glanced to Marley. "I think you'll need to wait out here."

Violet shrugged. "If you want company, the more, the merrier. We'll be done inside of a few minutes though. All I have to do is stick a needle in your arm and draw some blood. I do it all day long, so I'm pretty efficient."

Marley caught her eyes. "Up to you."

"I'm good. You wait here with Holly, and I'll be back in a few."

At that, Violet spun around and gestured to Lacey to

follow her. Violet strode quickly ahead of Lacy, her stride confident. Though she was on the short side, she came across as taller than she was by virtue of her strong, no-nonsense presence. Her almost-black hair was tied back with a neon green ribbon to match her shirt. Lacey wondered how come she'd never seen her around town before. "How long have you been in Diamond Creek?" Lacey asked as she followed Violet into a small exam room.

Violet threw a grin over her shoulder. "About a month. People keep asking me that, like they're confused how come they don't know me. I figure maybe after I've been here a decade, people might consider me local. I decided I wanted to work somewhere different. When I came across the ad here for a phlebotomist, I figured it'd be fun. I moved here from New York City, so this place is different to say the least. So far, so good though." She patted the seat on a chair. "Have a seat. Are you left handed or right handed?"

"Right handed."

"Okay, then put your left arm here. I do my best to make sure you won't walk out of here with soreness, but there's always a little. Can't stab someone and have it be completely pain free," Violet said matter-of-factly.

"What about acupuncture?" Lacey asked with a wink.

"Oh right. They do stab you with needles. I dunno. I've heard it doesn't hurt, but I have to find a vein and draw blood, so that's a little different."

Violet turned away and tapped the keyboard on a laptop on a counter just beside Lacey. "Okay, I have to confirm a few incredibly obvious details. I always say they might be obvious to you, but if it turned out we were running the wrong tests on the wrong person and labeled the blood incorrectly, we'd all wish we'd taken a few seconds to discuss the obvious. So, name and date of birth?"

"Lacey Adams. 3/4/1986."

"It says you're here for testing related to symptoms of Multiple Sclerosis. Is that correct?"

Violet's tone was calm and matter-of-fact. It contrasted sharply with the turmoil Lacey felt inside. When she didn't reply promptly, Violet glanced away from the computer screen to her. Her blue eyes, the color almost translucent, softened. She waited a few beats, her eyes watching Lacey carefully. "I'm guessing you're not too thrilled about this, huh?"

Lacey shrugged and aimed for nonchalant. "Who would be?" she asked rhetorically.

Violet's lips quirked. "No one I know, but some people are more used to dealing with medical stuff. If I had to guess, you strike me as the type who's been healthy as a horse. You're in great shape, so it's not hard to figure that out."

"Honestly, I've seen the doctor more in the last month than in the last decade. It's so frustrating," she said with a shake of her head.

"Frustrating's one way to put it. Maybe scary too." Violet paused and looked beyond Lacey for a long moment before her eyes flicked back. "Look, I just met you, so I hope you don't mind a little unsolicited feedback." At Lacey's subtle shake of her head, Violet continued. "I decided to be a phlebotomist because I had my blood drawn what felt like a million times when I was little. Some of the people who did it were great and some totally sucked at it. I had childhood leukemia, you know, blood cancer. That means blood draws out the wazoo. Anyway, I'm not telling you this because you care about why I do what I do, but because I get what it's like to wish things were different. Maybe it's not obvious, but I'm not exactly the laid back type. Being sick and in the hospital sucked, but it made me so much stronger. I can't say I know what it's like to have MS, but I know what it's like to be really damn sick and wish it would all go away. I promise, it won't make you weaker. You'll just get stronger in different ways."

Lacey stared at Violet. For the first time since she'd had an inkling of what might be happening to her, she felt like someone completely understood how she felt. The sense of relief that washed through her was so powerful, she sagged into the chair.

"You okay?" Violet asked. "I didn't mean to upset…"

"You didn't. You said just what I needed to hear today. I'm sure I'm still gonna have shitty days and be flat pissed if it turns out I have MS, but it's nice to feel like someone gets it. You know?"

Violet nodded emphatically.

"My family loves me and I know they're worried. My boyfriend is a doctor and he's all worried. It's not like it doesn't help, but it's just…I don't know. It's weird. All I know is I want these tests over so my doctor can rule out MS."

Violet's broad smile returned, and she patted the wide, flat armrest on the chair. "Then let's get this done."

As Violet quickly prepped the area on Lacey's arm, it occurred to Lacey she'd just called Quinn her boyfriend. It had rolled off her tongue like it was a fact. The prick of the needle brought her attention back to the moment. Violet quickly drew Lacey's blood and slowly removed the needle. With one hand, she swabbed the tiny pinprick on Lacey's arm, while she tapped the vial of blood and tightly sealed it with the other.

"You're all set," she said as she carefully placed a sticker with Lacey's name on it around the vial of blood.

Lacey stood up. She started to walk to the door and turned back. "Thanks for…uh…"

"Telling you my mini sob story about having leukemia?" Violet offered helpfully.

Lacey burst out laughing. "Yes, that."

"Anytime. If I see you again, you might get another pep talk."

At that, Lacey gave a little wave and turned to leave. As she walked down the hall to the waiting room, she felt much lighter than she'd expected.

* * *

QUINN STOOD in the middle of the office Dr. Daniels had escorted him into. It was dawning on Quinn that he would be working in full swing as a doctor within days. Dr. Daniels had cleared out his office in anticipation of Quinn's arrival, leaving only the furniture. Quinn spun in a circle, stopping to face the view. Coastal Medical Clinic was situated almost smack in the middle of downtown Diamond Creek on Harborside Road, which was a side street off of Main Street and close to Otter Cove Harbor. The office, about to become Quinn's, offered a view of a marshy field with Kachemak Bay beyond it. Quinn glanced behind him to notice the desk was facing the view. He grinned, realizing he could at least look up at this when he needed a break.

He strode out of the office and down the hallway. There were two exam rooms, a records room, and a break room that held a tiny refrigerator and a microwave, along with a small table and chairs. When he stepped into the waiting area, Donna Keller glanced up with a wide smile. Donna had been Dr. Daniel's office manager for twenty years and made the clinic run smoothly. According to Dr. Daniels, she wasn't planning to go anywhere. She had silver hair and bright brown eyes with a round, motherly presence.

"Dr. Daniels already left. He said for you to call him if you needed anything," she said.

"He did?"

Donna nodded, her smile widening. "He sure did. He said he mentioned the appointments for this week to you."

Quinn leaned against the counter surrounding Donna's desk. "He did, but I guess I thought maybe he'd be around some."

"Oh, he'll be around, but I don't think he plans to do any more work other than giving you a little guidance here and there. Trust me, he said he'd wait until you were here, but that man is seriously ready to retire!"

Quinn eyed Donna for a long moment and chuckled. "Right. He did say he'd be backing out as soon as I was up and running. I guess I didn't realize that meant today."

Donna laughed and shrugged. "Don't worry. I'm not going anywhere. He'll pop in here and there." Her smiled faded. "He's tired. He's got arthritis in his back and one of his hands. His mind might be sharp as a tack, but he can't be on his feet all day anymore. He was more than relieved to find you. I'll take care of the schedule. All you need to do is show up. Do you have anything to move into your office?"

"I've been traveling so much the last few years, I don't have much of anything. I'll bring some reference books in. I guess I should be glad he left the furniture," he said with a shake of his head.

Donna's warm smile returned. "You just tell me if you need anything for your office, and I'll get it."

The phone jingled cheerily just then, and she held up a finger as she tapped the button on her headset. After she greeted whoever was calling, she nodded while she was listening and then asked to put them on hold. Her eyes swung back to Quinn. "We have a little boy who broke his wrist. Can you see him right now, or should I send him to the hospital? It's one of our regular patients."

Quinn mentally nudged himself into doctor mode. He might have had a more gradual transition in mind, but there was no reason not to get started right away. "Tell them to come on down. I've got the lay of the land in the exam room, so I know we have what we need."

Donna beamed at him, clearly pleased he wasn't hesitating to leap in. Roughly a half an hour later, a mother stood by the exam table, watching carefully while Quinn fit a cast on her son's arm. Quinn had already x-rayed the boy's arm, confirming the suspected broken wrist, and set the break carefully. The little boy with his bright blonde hair and round blue eyes had managed to fall off the family's back deck while attempting to prove he could balance on the thin railing.

"Okay, Benny, you should be good to go," Quinn announced once he finished adjusting the air cast.

Benny lifted his arm experimentally. "I like the purple," he announced.

Sandy, his mother, rolled her eyes. "That would be what he notices," she said to Quinn. "How long did you say he needs to wear the cast again?"

"Let's schedule a follow up in three weeks. Kids heal pretty quickly, but I'd like to take a look and maybe switch out the cast then." Quinn looked to Benny. "Remember what I said, take it easy with that arm."

Benny nodded, his hair falling over his eyes as he did. Quinn followed them out to the reception area and bantered with Benny, while his mother scheduled the follow up appointment with Donna. After they left, Donna looked over at him. "Lacey and Marley Adams stopped by while you were busy. I told them you would be available after you finished up. They said to tell you they'd be at the brewery for lunch if you wanted to meet them." Donna paused, her eyes assessing. "So, are the rumors true about you and Lacey?"

When his eyes widened, Donna grinned. "You'd better get used to it. This town's tiny. When it comes to locals, rumors travel faster than a brush fire. Lacey's never been linked with anyone, so it's news if she's with you."

Quinn sighed and chuckled. "Willow Brook's about the

same size as Diamond Creek, so I'm familiar with the small town rumor mill. I guess I didn't realize anyone would even notice. I've hardly been here."

"Maybe so, but you've been staying with Lacey the whole time. Anyway, if you ask me, you couldn't find a better woman. You two are peas in a pod with all that backcountry wilderness stuff. I love Alaska and a good view, but that kind of hiking is just crazy if you ask me."

"I guess I'm glad you approve," he said slowly.

Donna' sly grin made him realize she'd just confirmed the answer to her question. He shook his head and pushed away from the counter. "Alright then. I think I'll take off to grab some lunch. I'll be back in a bit. I'd like to go over the schedule for next week and drag in what little I have for the office."

$\mathcal{L}$acey ran along Raven's Beach, savoring the icy air rushing into her lungs with each breath. It had been several weeks since Quinn had been officially here. She remained muddled if she tried to think about what she wanted. Yet, whenever they were together every moment was infused with an intimacy she couldn't ignore. He'd been so busy getting started at work that it was only this morning he mentioned needing to try to find his own place to live. She hadn't been able to bring herself to say what her heart wanted, which was for him not to go anywhere and stay with her. Once he'd left for work, she'd spent an hour online to plan and schedule some hiking trips next summer for customers. Her business was almost entirely conducted online, except for when she was personally guiding trips. After she finished up, she'd thrown on her winter running clothes and headed to the beach.

It continued to snow here and there, although winter hadn't taken a firm hold yet. They'd woken this morning to a frost-covered landscape. With an overcast sky and no sun breaking through to melt it, the heavy dusting of frost remained. It crunched under her feet as she slowed to a walk at the point where she usually turned back. The beach grasses were faded and gray under the frost. She paused to look out over the bay, which was calm at the moment. The mountains on the far side were partially obscured by the clouds. A raven called out from the trees nearby, and she spun away from the water to search it out.

Several ravens were perched in the spruce forest, chattering amongst themselves. She watched long enough to see the source of the chatter—a magpie darting among the trees and harassing the larger ravens. Even in the gray light, she could see the flash of its iridescent blue and green feathers. She laughed when a raven lifted from the trees and chased the magpie away. Undeterred, the magpie swooped back to the trees.

As she began her run back, she took stock, mentally scanning her body. Dr. Marshall had ruled out any other medical causes for Lacey's symptoms, but she was still holding off on a formal MS diagnosis. She wanted to confirm that the nerve damage stemmed from separate events. Lacey was still annoyed with the situation, although she was learning to tolerate the uncertainty. It helped to have Quinn confirm he agreed with Dr. Marshall's caution. She recalled Violet's words about how she'd become stronger in a different way. Lacey wasn't sure that's what she wanted, but she was trying to adjust. Problem was, as long as she didn't have an official diagnosis, she kept clinging to the hope that this cluster of episodes was nothing more than a blip that would never happen again.

At the moment, she felt like her old self—strong and powerful. She'd always loved running because of the high it gave her and the way it grounded her into the moment. Right now, all she knew was the feel of her feet pushing against the sand with each stride, the flex of her muscles and the rhythm of her breath. As more time had passed since her last episode, she'd become braver about returning to her old habits of running long distances. She figured as long as she had her phone, she'd be able to call for help if needed.

The fabled runner's high was coursing through her. Her mood light, she dug in and pushed herself to run harder. After roughly a half mile, one of her legs gave out abruptly. She'd been moving so fast, she couldn't catch her balance when she started to stumble and crashed onto the sand and rocks. Sharp pain shot through her arm where her elbow collided with a rock. She tried to clamber up, but her right leg wasn't cooperating at all. It felt like a dead weight. Unlike the other times, she had no warning—no preceding weakness and no tingling. Now that she'd fallen, the weakness was quite evident and her nerves tingled along the outside of her thigh.

She lay there for several minutes, the sand cold underneath her, before she slowly sat up. It wasn't impossible to do with her useless leg, but it was beyond annoying. Once again, her strength and physical fitness were failing her. She sat there and stared out over the water, the layers of gray well suited to her now-gloomy mood. Her runner's high had disappeared the second she crashed to the ground. She tried to take heart in Violet's words, but right now she just wanted to cry. Tears rolled down her cheeks. The ocean and mountains across blurred as she sat there. She didn't even have the energy to wipe her tears away. Her breath misted the air around her with every heave and sob. Alone on the empty beach with no one to hear, she cried and cried until the tears slowed and she was left wrung out.

Dragging her sleeve across her damp cheeks, she took stock. She experimented with lifting her leg, but it defied her. She could only move it incrementally. Her left leg felt completely normal though, and her vision was fine. She supposed she should count her blessings, but she wasn't really feeling it at the moment. She glanced around to find a raven perched on a piece of driftwood nearby, watching her curiously. She watched the raven in return until the bird hopped off the driftwood and took flight, returning to its friends in the trees. She was starting to get cold, so she pulled her phone out and stared at the screen.

She was torn over calling Quinn. On the one hand, she desperately wanted to soak in his strength and comfort. On the other, she didn't like how vulnerable she felt just now. Yet, she'd feel vulnerable no matter who she called for help. Her mother would fuss over her and worry like crazy. It would be the same with Marley. While Quinn would worry, he wasn't the type to fuss. Only he could offer the comfort she craved at the moment because it was a quite specific Quinn-craving.

If you were wondering how you felt about him... Her traitorous mind chose now to chime in. *Not now, okay. It's bad enough I've collapsed on the beach and am sick to death of not knowing for sure what the hell is wrong. I don't need to worry about whatever the hell is going on with Quinn too. Just sayin' maybe you should stop wrestling with how you feel about him.* Damn, the competing voices inside of her head could be headstrong.

With a mental shake, she tapped the screen and pulled up Quinn's name. In a second, the phone was ringing. He picked up on the third ring. "Hey, what's up?"

She froze, nervous to report she'd once again collapsed on the beach. She waited long enough that he spoke again. "Lace? You still there?"

"Yeah, yeah. I'm here. Are you busy?"

"I'm just finishing up on some paperwork if that counts as busy. I don't have any more appointments today though. Donna usually works one half day a week and today's her day for that, so we keep the afternoon clear."

"Oh, okay."

"You okay? You sound, I don't know, off."

"That might be because I went for a run and one of my legs stopped working again."

"What else is going on and where are you?" he asked, his tone sharp and abrupt.

She could practically see him shift gears. He was all focus and concern. "Not much else happening here unless you count the tide starting to come in."

"I'm on my way. Which beach?"

"Same one where I fell before," she said with a sigh. Her throat was tightening with tears again. Dammit, she did *not* want to cry again. She gulped in air and the feeling subsided.

"Aside from your leg, tell me how you feel."

She could hear his footsteps and then the sound of what she surmised was his car door. Just knowing he was on the way instantly soothed her inside.

"Nothing else. I don't have that weird blurry vision thing, and it's just my right leg. I probably bruised my elbow when I fell on a rock though."

"Okay, you're staying on the line until I get there."

She gripped the phone tightly in her hand, part of her chafing against needing anyone this much. "I don't need to stay on the line," she said, tears threatening again.

"I'm on my way. Just stay on the phone," he countered.

"Why?" Her voice rose a notch, and she flinched how churlish she sounded.

"Because I'm worried. That's all," he said, his voice softening.

Emotion tightened her throat, and she closed her eyes. The part of her that savored his protectiveness managed to shush her childish, argumentative side.

"Lace? You're not talking. Still with me?"

"Right here, not hanging up even if I kinda want to."

He chuckled at that. "Thanks for humoring me."

She got through the next few minutes with snippets of conversation about her surroundings. Quinn's office was downtown, so he was maybe ten minutes from the path leading to the beach. He must have set a new record to get there because she saw his form appear on the path just past five minutes from when she called.

* * *

QUINN SAW Lacey sitting on the sand, her bright purple jacket standing out in the gray light. In the short span of time since she'd called, his heart had been pounding for all the wrong reasons. He could tell himself intellectually she'd be okay, but it didn't seem to translate to his heart. She'd taken up residence there and all he knew was he needed to make sure she was okay. He broke into a run. "Almost there," he said into the phone.

"I know. I can see you," she said wryly.

The fact she could summon a little humor eased his concern. She was further down the beach this time than she had been before. Close to a mile he guessed. Only when he reached her did he start to relax inside. She glanced up, her green eyes bright against her skin. The look of relief in her eyes was so clear, all he wanted to do was wrap her in his arms and promise her it would be okay. He would make sure it would. Yet, right now, it was cold and the tide was coming in. He needed to get her off the beach and to Dr. Marshall's office as soon as humanly possible.

"You can hang up now," she said. She started to smile, but it wobbled and she looked down.

His heart clenched. He slipped his phone in his pocket and eased down by her side on one knee. The sand was icy cold, and he realized Lacey was probably freezing. He stroked a palm down her spine and felt the subtle shivers running through her.

"How long have you been sitting here?"

She lifted one shoulder in a shrug. "Not long. Maybe ten minutes or so before I called you. Please don't tell me I should've called right away. I was hoping it would pass."

He took a breath, trying to wrestle the emotions crashing through him. This was so not him. While this might not be a full-blown crisis, under usual circumstances when he was assisting a friend or customer on trips if they were injured, he'd be entirely focused on what needed to happen. Instead, all he could think about was wrapping Lacey in his arms and wiping the guarded, fearful look in her eyes away.

He mentally shook himself, forcing his attention to what needed to happen. "We need to get you off this beach before you get much colder. Let's see if you can walk with my support. Okay?"

At her nod, he eased his arm around her back. She shifted onto her left hip and slowly adjusted her good leg, so the foot was planted on the ground. With him holding most of her weight, they slowly stood. When he glanced down, her mouth was in a tight line and her breath came in short pants.

"Okay?" he asked.

She nodded tightly, keeping her eyes averted. He moved to her weak side and slipped his arm around her waist, holding firmly. They started to walk, but it was clearly difficult for her. After several moments, she stopped.

"Give me a sec."

Her shivering had increased. Knowing how hard she tended to push herself when she ran, Quinn figured she'd worked up a sweat before her leg gave out, which meant her body was chilled from the damp sweat now. He looked ahead, calculating how long it would take them to reach his car. A cold wind had begun to gust off the bay, whipping across the beach.

He glanced to her. Strands of her auburn hair had come loose from her ponytail and blew around her face. She looked weary and frustrated. He didn't wait to ask and turned, quickly lifting her in his arms.

"Hey! I can make it," she said, her voice lilting.

"I'm sure you can, but we've got a ways to go. It's freezing and I want to get you to Dr. Marshall's office now."

To his surprise, she didn't argue. He adjusted her in his arms with one arm under her hips and the other at the bend of her knees. She looped her arms around his shoulders, managing a weak grin. "Fine, I'll let you be all manly and carry me."

He chuckled, relieved she wasn't arguing. However, her lack of resistance also concerned him because it told him a lot about how weak she must be feeling. It tore at his heart to see the strong woman he knew feeling this weak. He began walking with her held against his chest. She was quiet after that and eventually relaxed into his hold. With each step, his heart squeezed a little tighter. He needed to get her through this afternoon and somehow figure out what to do with what was happening between them. He didn't know if his heart could take anything less than everything. He was damning his own fear of simply trying to talk to her, as Marley had suggested so long ago now. Each time he considered it, he'd get wrapped up in the moment, or avoid it for fear of messing up how good it felt.

He eventually reached his car and opened the passenger door. Once he'd deposited her in the seat, he carefully closed the door and climbed in on the driver's side. He started the car and immediately turned the heat up. She was visibly shivering now, and he wanted her warm as quickly as possible.

"Anything you need from your car?" he asked, glancing to her.

"Just my purse. I'll call Marley and see if she can pick up my car."

"You do that while I grab your purse."

When he returned to his car and handed her purse over, she set it on her lap. "Marley's on the way. Let's get to Dr. Marshall's and get this over with," she said with a heavy sigh.

A few hours later, Quinn walked at Lacey's side to her cabin. A light snow had started to fall. Dr. Marshall had given Lacey another injection of corticosteroids and insisted she immediately schedule another MRI. Quinn was close to certainty Lacey had MS, but he respected Dr. Marshall's caution in formally making the diagnosis. If anything, he wondered if she was being thorough beyond thorough to ensure Lacey didn't hold doubts. While Lacey had repeatedly expressed her frustration with the process, he knew her well enough to know she'd hold onto questions as well.

At the moment, it was clear the corticosteroids were starting to help. She was able to put some weight on her right leg and her limp was much less pronounced. He resisted the urge to help her up the stairs because it was clear she wanted to manage on her own. Their footsteps left a path in the dusting of snow on her deck. Once they were inside, he didn't bother to ask if she wanted him to start a fire and immediately took care of it. After he closed the door to the woodstove, glancing through the glass to confirm the flames were taking hold in the tinder under the logs, he looked over to see her waiting by the stairs.

Electricity arced through the air between them. Against all reason, he wanted her badly right now. Her eyes darkened and she angled her head to the side. "I might need help getting up the stairs. I need a shower like crazy, but I don't want to be stupid. Three steps outside was no big deal, but there's thirteen here," she said gesturing to the stairs beside her. The fact she was asking for his help again did strange things to his heart. His need to protect her drew him closer and confused him—this wasn't how he was accustomed to seeing her.

In a flash, he was at her side, sliding his arm around her waist. He navigated the stairs carefully with her, relieved to sense her increased strength since earlier. In minutes, she was peeling off her clothes and stepping into the shower. He couldn't resist joining her and followed her into the steamy shower. She was covered in soap. He wasn't sure if it was sensible to want her right now, but that was how powerful the pull to her was. He ran his hands down her sides, savoring the feel of her skin, slick under his touch. She slowly turned in his arms and leaned her head back to let the water rinse the shampoo out of her hair. When she tilted her head up again, she stroked her palm down his chest to curl around his quite obvious arousal.

He dipped his head and caught her lips in a kiss, pouring everything into it—his overwhelming desire for her, his desperate need to protect her from anything and every-thing, and his need to meld himself as close as physically possible to her. Their kiss went wild—tongues tangling and teeth clashing. He tore his lips free and licked and nipped his way down her neck. He held her firmly with one arm to make sure she didn't lose her balance. He might be almost out of his mind with lust for her, but a tiny corner of him remembered her strength wasn't one hundred percent at the moment. He dragged his free hand up her abdomen to trace circles on the skin of her breasts. When her head fell back against the tile, he leaned forward and swirled his tongue around a nipple before sucking it into his mouth and biting down softly. Her hands threaded into his wet hair and gripped as he alternated between her nipples, lick-ing, sucking and nipping. His cock was so hard, he was on the verge of coming right then and there. He eased a hand under her knee and slowly lifted her against him.

Her eyes opened and slammed into his. He couldn't look away from her, the depth of feeling he held inside reflected back to him in her gaze. He adjusted her weight and positioned his cock at her entrance. When he held still for a moment, she shifted her hips restlessly against him. He sank inside of her, seating himself fully within her creamy clench. She gasped, her nails digging into his back. Her channel throbbed around him, and he didn't know how long he could hold back.

With the shower wall to help him hold her, he eased a hand between them and circled it over her clit. Her eyes closed and her channel started to pulse around his cock. He drew back incrementally and rocked his hips into the cradle of hers. Within seconds, she cried out, her entire body going taut and shuddering against his. He let go, driving one more time deeply inside of her, his own release thundering through him. His head fell into the dip of her shoulder and he held her tightly. With the hot water raining down around them, he slowly caught his breath and lifted his head. She opened her eyes, a slow smile curling her lips.

CHAPTER 17

*L*acey rolled her head to the side to look out the windows. Dawn was just breaking, the light wispy and thin rays of sun breaking through the clouds in orange and gold. The landscape was blanketed with snow. The spruce trees were bright green under the dusting. She rolled her head to the other side to see Quinn's amber hair mussed. He was still asleep, his breathing even and steady. His palm was resting on her abdomen as he slept curled toward her. Her heart tightened as she contemplated yesterday afternoon and evening. He'd given far more than the comfort she sought when she'd called him for help. She was starting to feel like she'd let things go too far. He meant too much, but she didn't enjoy feeling like she needed anyone, and she was feeling dangerously close to needing him in more ways than one.

With a mental shake, she rolled her head away and stared at the ceiling, idly counting the knots in the pine. She mentally scanned her body and was relieved to find she felt only lingering weakness in her right leg. Those injections Dr. Marshall gave her were miraculous. Problem was, she hated needing them. Dr. Marshall had said she'd like her to come back in later this week—again—to discuss preventative treatment options. A huge part of her wanted to simply ignore the whole thing, but reality was making it hard to do that.

With a sigh, she turned on her side and started to sit up. She felt Quinn's touch on her back, a slow pass down her spine. Dear God. All he had to do was touch her and her body hummed. Her skin prickled in the wake of his touch. She closed her eyes at the intensity of feeling that rose within and gulped in air. That's how bad it was. She was on the verge of drowning in emotion and sensation.

"Mornin'," he said, his voice gravelly with sleep.

She eased onto her hip and angled to face him. "Good morning. I was trying not to wake you up."

He shrugged a shoulder and slowly sat up, the covers falling to his waist and revealing his sculpted chest and abs. Her mouth went dry and need tightened inside of her. This was getting ridiculous. She needed to get this crazy, out of control attraction to him under control.

"I'm usually up early. You know that," he said. "Coffee?"

She couldn't help but smile. "Of course."

Over the next half hour, she swung between wanting to relax and enjoy the morning and feeling irritated with herself for letting her feelings spiral out of hand so quickly. She couldn't help but think she'd have kept it together if all this stupid medical stuff weren't happening. It felt as if her life had been shaken up, and she was grasping at whatever she could to hold on. Quinn's proximity and their incredibly inconvenient desire made him an easy person to hold onto.

She drained her coffee cup and gathered herself together. She'd act normal and get this in hand. "You mentioned you were going to start looking for a place to stay yesterday. Any leads yet?" Most of her hated asking the question, but the part of her that she used to rely on—the strong, didn't need anyone part—held firm.

She couldn't read his eyes when he glanced up. They were carefully blank. "Donna gave me a few suggestions the other day. I haven't had much time to make any calls."

"Oh. Well, I was just curious."

He was quiet for a long moment. He stared down at the counter and traced a circle around his coffee mug. When he glanced up, he looked determined. "I'm not sure now's a good time, but maybe we should talk."

"About what?" she asked, her heart pounding and anxiety blooming in her chest.

His amber eyes held hers. "Us."

Stubbornness rose inside. She didn't want to talk. Not now. She wanted time to think, to sort things out on her own—to feel like her life wasn't rampaging wildly out of her control.

"What about us?"

His eyes widened. "Do I need to point out the obvious? There're all kinds of 'us' things that have changed in the last month or so. I thought maybe we should try to talk."

She shook her head sharply. "I can't do this right now. I'm not going to pretend like nothing's happening, but I need some time. There's too much going on."

His eyes shuttered, and she felt the distance viscerally, which instantly made her heart ache with longing. She had to hold herself back from flinging herself into his arms.

Somehow they got through the next little while with Quinn getting ready for work, and her putzing around the house doing mindless tasks. For the first time in days, he didn't kiss her goodbye. He gave a small wave at the door and walked out into the snow. She went upstairs, relieved her weak leg felt close to normal. She most certainly wasn't up for asking for help getting up the stairs right now.

When she came downstairs again after showering and

dressing, she glanced out the window and saw he'd shoveled the deck and a path to her car. He'd also brushed all the snow off her car, which Marley had dropped off yesterday afternoon. She sat down on the bottom stair and burst into tears.

* * *

QUINN WAS RELIEVED he had such a busy day. Donna had booked him straight through, which didn't offer him the opportunity to dwell on this morning. The last patient left for the day and he plunked down at his desk to get through some charting. He'd been relieved to learn Dr. Daniels had already invested in an electronic health record system and even more relieved that it happened to be a system he'd used during his residency. As he clicked through and entered a few notes, he heard footsteps coming down the hall and Donna appeared in the doorway. Her brown eyes twinkled with her smile as she leaned against the doorframe.

"Well, today turned out to be busier than I planned. I accidentally double booked you twice and didn't even catch it! That almost never happens but with transitioning all of Dr. Daniel's appointments over to you in the system, there were a few mix-ups. Thanks for being such a good sport about it."

He leaned back in his chair and grinned. "I didn't even notice. I just kept moving onto the next patient. Gotta say, I was wondering if it was like this all the time."

Donna shrugged. "It's always busy, but today was a little busier than usual. Now that I've got most of the appointments and patients under you in the system, it should be fine. I have a few left to transfer over, but none of them have any appointments scheduled. I saved those for last. So...how you doing now that you've made it through a few weeks here?"

"Good. The doctor part applies no matter where I work, but I don't think I'd manage here without you to take care of everything else," he said with a wry grin. He paused, considering Lacey's question this morning about whether he'd looked into getting his own place. "You mentioned a place I should check out to rent. Can you refresh my memory on that?"

"My daughter and her husband have a place they rent out every winter after the tourists are gone, but they've already found a renter. Let me ask around and see what else I can find out for you."

"That'd be great. I've been so busy, I haven't had much of a chance to think about it."

He sensed Donna's curiosity, but he wasn't up for questions right now. She knew he'd been staying with Lacey and was likely wondering about that. He forced the conversation onto other topics. "Dr. Daniels mentioned he'd be stopping by sometime this week. You happen to know when that might be? I wanted to follow up with him on a patient."

Donna quickly pulled out her phone and called Dr. Daniels. When she got his voice mail, she all but ordered him to stop by soon. When she hung up, she glanced out the window behind Quinn. "I need to get going before that snow gets too heavy. You should too," she said with a warning glance. "I'll see you in the morning." At that, she gave a wave and turned to walk down the hall again, flicking lights off in the exam rooms as she did.

He heard the front door close and then silence. He swiveled in his chair and looked outside. Darkness was falling and snow along with it. With the office quiet around him, he slowly walked through. It was strange to realize this was where he would be for the foreseeable future. Even stranger to contemplate that Dr. Daniels hired him with the hope Quinn would eventually buy him out and the practice would be Quinn's entirely. When Quinn had applied for this position, he'd been thinking he loved Diamond Creek and he had a good friend in the area. Lacey being the good friend in question. That was before the answering desire in her eyes fanned the flames of his own long-buried desire. Now, he was facing much more than desire. He loved her, and he didn't know if or when she might be ready to face what lay between them. What he hadn't counted on was that he might reach the point where he was now. He didn't think he could allow himself to tumble deeper into what he had with her. If he wanted to salvage the possibility of friendship with her, which he desperately did, he needed to take a step back.

He stood in the middle of the dark and empty waiting room and looked out into the snowy parking lot. With a sigh, he quickly walked back to his office and turned everything off before tossing on his jacket. He drove to Lacey's cabin with the snow swirling around him, wondering how to talk to her. When he reached the drive to her cabin, he hesitated and made the quick decision to drive past it to the lodge.

Moments later, he tugged the heavy front door open and kicked the snow off his boots before stepping inside. He glanced around at the cluster of customers waiting to be seated and experienced a moment of hesitation. He didn't know why he was here, other than to buy some time before he faced Lacey. As he stood there, he heard someone call his name and glanced behind him to find Marley walking toward him with Holly in her arms and Gage a few steps behind her on the phone.

"Hey Quinn! So nice to see you," Marley said, giving him a side-hug. "Is Lacey with you?"

"Great to see you too," he said, striving for a casual tone even though he felt twisted up inside over Lacey. "Just stopped by to grab some dinner from the buffet." His statement was half-true, considering that once he'd made the decision to come here, he had figured he'd get some dinner.

Marley's eyes, so similar to Lacey's, narrowed when he didn't reply to her question about Lacey. While Marley wasn't as headstrong as Lacey, she also wasn't one to back down. "And Lacey?"

He shrugged. "I'm not sure. I'll probably find out after I get a bite here."

Gage happened to finish his call at the moment, saving Quinn from further grilling by Marley. "Hey man, how's it going?" he asked with an arch of a brow and a clap on Quinn's shoulder.

"Alright. How about you?"

Gage flashed a grin. "Pretty damn good now that the snow's starting to stick. I love every season, but winter's my favorite."

Gage curled an arm across Marley's shoulders and started walking, gesturing for Quinn to follow. As he followed them, he quickly slipped his phone out and texted Lacey to tell her he was stopping for dinner. They threaded their way through the crowded restaurant to the back corner booth. Once they were seated, the next little bit passed quickly with a waitress serving them drinks and a swing by the buffet and back. After Gage ably got Holly settled in a high chair and took turns with bites of his own food and offering bites to Holly, Marley glanced across the table to Quinn.

"Okay, Lacey's not here and something's up. Spill it," she ordered.

Quinn's chest knotted, but he managed to finish chewing his bite of food and take a sip of water. He knew Marley was only asking because she cared, but he didn't know if it was okay to talk to her about any of this. He glanced between her and Gage. Gage caught his eyes and lifted one shoulder in a shrug. "No escaping this."

Quinn ran a hand through his hair and looked over at Marley. "I tried to take your advice and talk to Lacey this morning. She told me she can't talk right now, that there's too much going on."

Marley eyed him for a long moment before she set her fork down and sighed. "Seriously?"

"Of course I'm serious. Anyway, the thing is I don't know what the hell to do because I'm not so sure I can deal with this dragging out if she'd rather things ended. We might have already gone past the point of no return with our friendship, but I'd like to try to salvage it if I can. I'm thinking maybe it's best if I find another place to stay in the meantime." He leaned his head against the back of the booth. "Ah hell. I knew it wasn't a good idea to let things go this far, but I couldn't seem to stop it."

His heart literally ached with his chest tight and his breath short. He forced himself to take a slow breath and rolled his head from side to side, easing the tension bundled there.

"You can stay here," Marley said firmly. "Lacey will come to her senses, or I'll make her."

Gage threw his head back with a laugh. He paused in feeding Holly to glance at her, his eyes wide. "You can't *make* anyone come to their senses."

Marley punched him lightly on the shoulder. "Maybe not, but I can try." She glanced back to Quinn, her eyes sobering. "You really love her, don't you?"

Quinn noticed Gage was purposefully busying himself by slowly feeding Holly bites of macaroni. Quinn didn't much care to hide his feelings, but he appreciated Gage's efforts to make it seem like he couldn't hear absolutely everything they were saying. He met Marley's eyes straight on and took a deep breath. "Seems to be the case. I mean, she's been one of my best friends for years. When this, I don't even know what to call it, started with us, I wasn't sure it was a great idea because I didn't want to blow up our friendship. Now, I'm afraid we might."

Gage set the spoon down and wiped Holly's mouth before handing her a stuffed turtle, which she immediately latched onto. His eyes flicked from Marley to Quinn. Quinn didn't know Gage all that well yet, but it was more than obvious not much slipped past him. "It won't come to that," he said firmly. "I've seen the way Lacey looks at you, and, trust me, you're far more than just a friend to her." His eyes canted sideways to Marley, his mouth curling in a grin, before his gaze swung back to Quinn. "Marley might not appreciate what I'm about to say, but Lacey's stubborn as hell. Don't let that get in your way."

Marley rolled her eyes. "Fine. My sister might be kind of stubborn, but it's the best kind. Just..." she paused, worry entering her gaze "...give her a little time. Do you feel like you need to stay somewhere else? Will that make it messier?"

Quinn shrugged. "I don't know what's best, but I don't know if I can keep my own sanity if I try to muddle along like nothing's going on when that seems to be what she wants me to do."

Marley traced the beads of moisture on her water glass and sighed. "I get it. Any news from her doctor?"

"She ordered another MRI yesterday after what happened and..."

Marley cut him off. "What happened yesterday?"

Quinn silently swore. He should've guessed Lacey might have avoided mentioning her collapse on the beach yesterday. He looked over at Marley and ran a hand through his hair again. "I guess she didn't mention that to you, huh?"

Marley shook her head sharply. "She asked me to pick

up her car because she was catching a ride with you, but that's all she said. What happened?"

"She was running on the beach again and her leg gave out. She called me, so I went to get her and dragged her straight to Dr. Marshall's office."

"I swear, I wish she'd wasn't so damn determined never to ask anyone for help. I guess I should be relieved she called you, but it pisses me off she hasn't even mentioned this to me."

Quinn shrugged. "Look, she's just trying to get through this. I don't think she was purposefully hiding it, but it's not fun to give updates on stuff like this. Give her time to get used to it."

Marley sighed and leaned back. "I know, I know. I just wish she'd notice that there's only one person she happens to be comfortable asking for help. You. If there's anything that tells me how she feels about you, it's that."

* * *

LACEY FLIPPED through the channels on television and couldn't keep her eyes from veering to the clock on the wall behind the woodstove. She'd started a fire and settled in to try to take her mind off wondering where Quinn was. It wasn't like he needed to report back to her, but after this morning, she was worried he'd already found another place to stay and hadn't even bothered to tell her. She'd spent most of the day valiantly trying to keep her mind off of him by busying herself with work and cleaning her house. Winter was a quiet time for her when it came to work. She mostly scheduled summer trips online here and there and did some planning for equipment needs. In short order, she'd run out of official work to do, so she'd thrown herself into cleaning the house, completely ignoring Dr. Marshall's recommendation to take it easy. By the time the light had faded to gray and the snow started falling in earnest, her cabin was sparkling clean. Quinn hadn't called or texted and still hadn't come home.

This isn't his home. You made that perfectly clear this morning. Her mind taunted her with the truth about the effect of her words earlier. *But I want it to be his home.* Her heart gave a hard thump, and anxiety knotted in her chest. She couldn't let herself go there now. It was too much to face how much he'd come to mean. Every time she thought about it, she considered that she wasn't the woman he'd always known. She wasn't strong, independent and invincible anymore. She wasn't silly enough to think she'd ever been invincible, but she'd felt like she could charge at anything that came her way. Needing someone the way she'd needed Quinn yesterday was such an unfamiliar feeling, she didn't know how to navigate it. She didn't know how to reconcile that with trying to let this thing between them be real.

Oh it's real. It's already very real. She swatted that thought away and changed the channel. Her eyes quickly bounced beyond the television to the snow glittering under the outside lights as it fell steadily.

CHAPTER 18

Quinn stood in Lacey's kitchen and poured a cup of coffee. After a few sips, he felt halfway human, although his heart hurt and his stomach was churning like mad. All the coffee did was wipe the cobwebs out of his brain after a crappy night's sleep. He'd arrived home late last night to realize the text he'd thought he'd sent to Lacey telling her he was grabbing dinner had never left his phone. He must've missed the send button when he dashed it off last night. Lacey had been sound asleep upstairs, so he'd crawled quietly into bed beside her. He'd woken this morning with her draped all over him. With his body thrumming with need and his cock throbbing, he'd slowly untangled himself and headed straight for a chilly shower. Much as he could hardly bear the thought of sleeping without Lacey, this morning reinforced why he needed to create some space. He couldn't take much more of this and have his heart survive it.

A few minutes later, she came downstairs, her auburn hair damp and her jade eyes bright in the gray, snowy light. His heart clenched at the sight of her. She took his breath away in more ways than one. She held her phone up. "Just got your text. I'm guessing you thought you sent it last night?"

"Good guess. Sorry 'bout that."

"No problem," she said, her tone guarded. "Thanks for shoveling off the deck and my car yesterday."

"Of course. Coffee's ready if you want some."

She stepped immediately to the cabinet, pulled out a mug and filled it. The space between them felt stilted and heavy with unexpressed feelings. He steeled himself to say what he knew had to be said before he lost his mind and they lost the good friendship between them.

"Lace, I, uh... I've been thinking. Maybe it's best if I stayed somewhere else right now. It sounds like we might be on different wavelengths, and I don't want to blow things up worse than we already have."

She didn't look at him, her eyes studiously staring out the windows. She swallowed, the sound loud in the quiet room. His heart was banging against his ribs. He wanted to take his words back. Finally, she looked back at him, pain glimmering in the depths of her gaze. "You don't need..." She paused for a breath. "I don't want you to..." Her words trailed off, and she swallowed again, her eyes canting down to where she was tracing her fingertip along the edge of the counter.

His heart leapt at her words, hope flaring inside. Then, she shook her head sharply. "Okay. I understand," she said, her words firmer this time.

* * *

LACEY HURRIED from Dr. Marshall's office to her car. It was late afternoon and another snowstorm was blowing in. Autumn, which had been making a slow bow, had hurried off the stage with winter roaring in to replace it. It had snowed almost every other day since Quinn moved out. She jumped into her car to start it and bounced back out to brush the snow off while the car warmed up. Snow blew in a swirl around her, the wind indecisive about which direction it wanted to blow and blowing every which way as a result.

Moments later, she climbed back into her car, snow whirling in with her. The heat had barely made a dent, although it was blowing mightily on the highest setting. She leaned her head back and sighed. Dr. Marshall had finally diagnosed Lacey with MS this afternoon. All the emotions Lacey had been battling over Quinn had worn her out. She had no idea how she'd gotten through today's appointment without falling apart, but she dredged up every ounce of internal strength and held it together while Dr. Marshall discussed preventative treatment options. She'd sent Lacey off with information to review and scheduled a follow up appointment within a few days.

Lacey sat there, shivering in the icy air, and wished upon wish she had more courage. Quinn had moved to the lodge temporarily while he looked for his own place to live. Marley had stopped by yesterday, ostensibly for a casual visit, although Lacey could tell Marley was worried about her. Lacey couldn't bring herself to admit she missed Quinn so much it hurt, so when Marley had asked about Quinn, Lacey had sidestepped and stayed vague. For once, she was relieved to talk about her pending appointment with Dr. Marshall and the results of her latest MRI. Every time she thought of Quinn, as she did now, her body recoiled against the reverberating emotional pain. She'd gone and done the stupidest thing ever, and she couldn't figure out how to fix it without feeling more vulnerable and exposed than she already did.

Quinn, being the decent guy he was, had already called and texted, his tone reminiscent of how it had been before she'd known him so intimately that it seared her soul. She knew he was trying to get them back on the footing of their once solid friendship, but she chafed against it. She wanted to spin back to where they'd been, but she was afraid Quinn wouldn't allow it unless she actually faced up to how much he meant to her. That meant tapping into a vein of fear she hadn't realized ran so deep within her.

Her whole life, she'd thrived on being strong and independent and not needing anyone. She loved her family and friends, but she flew solo through life, touching down only occasionally. Life, being the jokester it was, seemed to have decided she was due for a reality check in more ways than one. First, she was being forced to face up to her physical limitations and the reality she'd have to find a way to define herself within a different context. From what Dr. Marshall had offered, treatment options were available that would offer ways for her to prevent these episodes that brought her to her knees. She'd also shared there were some new treatment approaches through stem-cell transplants of Lacey's own stem cells that showed promise for completely halting the progression of MS if hers turned out to be more severe. Those details aside, Lacey no longer felt like she lived up to her old childhood nickname. She wasn't feeling too Brawny anymore.

Then, there was Quinn. She couldn't have known that giving into her desire for him would mean her heart would entwine itself so tightly to him, she couldn't find a way to let go. She needed him like the very air she breathed, and she was terrified of what that meant. It was bad enough to have the core of how she defined herself—strong, powerful, beyond the reach of needing anyone for anything—shake under the reality of a new medical diagnosis. Even worse, she felt emotionally fragile and tossed asunder by how quickly and deeply she'd fallen for Quinn.

A tear rolled down her cheek, cool against her skin. She

wiped it away and straightened in her seat. The snow was picking up its pace, already starting to pile up on her windshield again. She turned on her windshield wipers and tugged her seatbelt on before easing her car forward and making her way home through the falling darkness. When she arrived at her small cabin, its red roof the only spot of color in the snowy dusk, she trudged through the snow on her way inside. She immediately realized she hadn't stocked the small wood rack inside and had to turn around and go back out into the snow. She brushed the woodpile off and trekked in and out to fill the rack inside. With the wind howling, she started a fire and plunked down on the couch to watch television. A few months ago, she'd have been perfectly content. Tonight, she missed Quinn like crazy.

Her phone beeped, indicating a text had arrived. She snagged it off the table by the couch and glanced down to see a text from Quinn.

Roads aren't so great. Just checking to make sure you made it home okay.

Her heart squeezed, and she had to force herself to breathe before she replied.

Yup. Safe and sound.

There was so much more she wanted to say, most specifically she wanted to beg him to come back to the little cocoon they'd been living in at her cabin. Her rather monstrous pride held her back. He seemed to be managing okay with this whole 'back to friends' thing, so she'd have to find it in her to do the same. Problem was, she wasn't so sure she could pull it off.

QUINN CLOSED his laptop and glanced at his watch. Another busy day was done. Donna had left a few minutes ago, leaving him alone in the quiet office. He'd come to savor the few minutes he spent at the end of the day in the office. From the moment he arrived until the last patient left, his days were filled. He was finding he thoroughly enjoyed a general medical practice like this, mostly because every day involved a wild variety of challenges. He stood from his desk and walked to the front of the office. Snow was falling lightly again. Winter had stopped its teasing and firmly taken hold the last few weeks. His mind wandered to Lacey. Truthfully, any moment he wasn't entirely preoccupied with something else, his thoughts went straight to her.

It had been a full two weeks since he'd ended his temporary stay with her. He was looking in earnest for his own place to live, but had yet to find one. Marley and Gage insisted he could continue to stay at the lodge, although he'd been worried it was impinging on Lacey's frequency of visits there until Marley had shared Lacey was making a point to only stop by when he was at work. Marley was firm in her belief that he and Lacey were meant to be. Given that Lacey seemed barely able to tolerate seeing him, Quinn wasn't so sure about that. He'd made efforts to try to act the way he would've when they were just friends and hadn't nearly singed themselves on the fire burning between them.

He'd seen Lacey only once in two weeks, and he missed her every moment of every day. He watched the snow fall softly and wondered how to break through this impasse with her. He wished he could see into her heart and know what she wanted. Since that wasn't possible, he gnawed on his own feelings and tried to rein them in. To make matters worse, he couldn't stop worrying about her. He hadn't heard a peep about her latest medical tests. As the friends they'd once been, she'd have called him and peppered him with questions. Her silence concerned him. Either she was avoiding him, which was painful to consider, or she was struggling with whatever the results were.

As he stood there wondering, his phone vibrated in his

pocket. He slipped it out and saw an unfamiliar number. Not really caring who it was since it wasn't Lacey, he answered.

"Quinn here."

"Quinn, it's Rita Marshall. Do you have a minute?"

Feeling as if the universe had read his mind, he nodded before he realized she couldn't see him nodding. "Sure do," he belatedly replied. "What's up?"

Dr. Marshall quickly summarized a case and sought his feedback. After they finished discussing that, she moved on. "I want you to know I wouldn't normally ask, but I have a release on file to talk with you and I'm concerned about Lacey. Has she spoken with you about how she's doing?"

His stomach knotted with tension and his pulse jumped up a notch. It was not a good sign to have Lacey's doctor wondering how she was doing. "No, uh, she hasn't. Is everything okay?"

"Medically speaking, I've confirmed an MS diagnosis based on the last MRI. She and I met to review the results. I went over some preventative treatment options and scheduled a follow up. That was roughly two weeks ago, and she canceled yet another appointment today. My receptionist told me each time she's canceled, she just says something else came up, but I'm getting the feeling she's avoiding it at this point. I don't mean to bother you, but I thought I'd ask."

Quinn's gut churned with concern about Lacey. He forced himself to breathe slowly and answer calmly. "No problem. Feel free to call again if you need to. I'll try to check in and see what's going on. Obviously, it would be good for her to get started on a preventative course." He had a million other things he wanted to say, but they weren't for Dr. Marshall, so he held his tongue.

"That'd be great. I'll keep trying to reschedule with her in the meantime." At that, she hung up.

He slowly lowered the phone. His mind spun with

worry. As frustrated as he knew Lacey to be about her symptoms, it wasn't like her to avoid something like this. Reflexively, he tapped his phone screen and pulled up her name. In seconds, the phone was ringing. After several rings, he got her voice mail. He left a message asking her to call back and snagged his jacket off the hook inside the hallway closet and stepped out into the snowy evening.

He couldn't stop himself from driving to her cabin, galvanized by his concern. All the feelings he'd been trying to tamp down and wrestle into submission flared high. She was so much more than a friend now and damn if he knew what to do about it. It was becoming painfully obvious that his attempt to create space and let his feelings cool down had only illuminated just how impossible that might be. He turned into the winding drive that led to her cabin, his heart dropping when he saw the small parking area in front was empty.

CHAPTER 19

*L*acey stared through her windshield at a snowflake drifting lazily down. A small gust of wind caught it and spun the fluffy bit of snow in a circle before it landed against the glass and skidded sideways. The circle of light cast by her headlights illuminated the snow falling around her. Moments ago, her leg had gone tingly and weak. When she tried to push on the brakes, her foot slipped off the pedal and her car had bounced gently into the ditch. She rested her head against the seat and berated herself for blowing off her appointments with Dr. Marshall. All she'd needed to do was go in and discuss her options for preventative treatment and maybe this particular moment wouldn't be happening. She couldn't seem to face anything right now.

Quinn loomed in her mind, and she beat back the urge to call him. She'd moved past her silly pride, but he'd kept his distance. Now, she was wondering if he felt anywhere close to the way she did. If he could so easily step back, it was hard to believe he did. As for her, damn it all, she was full bore in love with him. His absence sharpened her long-

191

ing. Each day that passed, she missed him even more. Her realization about her feelings had come in a flash when he'd sent another one of his friendly, casual texts. She was coming to despise how hard he was trying to normalize things between them when all she wanted was to dive back to where they'd been.

Um, is now the time to obsess about Quinn? It's snowing, it's winter, it's dark and your car's in a ditch. Maybe you should call someone.

Lacey laughed aloud with no one but her to hear. Her laugh quieted as quickly as it came. She should call someone. There was only one person she wanted to call and that was Quinn. Yet, even if she'd managed to get over it and admit her feelings to herself, she wasn't feeling great about seeing him like this. It seemed like he'd been bailing her out of a few too many situations lately. Emotion welled inside and a tear rolled down her cheek, followed by another and another. In the muted quiet of her car with the snow and wind blowing around her, her phone squawked like a crow. She'd changed her ringer to that after watching Holly's glee at a pair of crows calling to each other while they swooped in the sky outside the windows at the lodge.

She fished her phone out of her pocket and answered without glancing at the screen.

"Hello?"

"Lace, it's Quinn. I stopped by your place and noticed you weren't home yet. I, uh, guess I was just calling to make sure you were okay."

As soon as he spoke, her heart started pounding wildly in her chest and flutters twirled in her belly. A pang shot through her entire being. She missed him *so, so* much.

She must've been quiet a few beats too long because he spoke again. "Lace, you there?"

Her heart clenched at the nickname he used for her. Even before she'd walked into the fire of desire between them and fallen so deep into love with him, he'd been the only person to ever call her Lace. She mentally pulled herself together. "I'm here."

"You sound funny. Is everything okay?"

She almost burst into laughter and tears at once. Everything was so not okay. She'd been too prideful to face her feelings and pushed him away. She needed to make it right, but she didn't know how and she was terrified to find out he might not return her feelings. Yet, there were more immediate issues to address, namely the fact she wasn't going anywhere soon unless someone came to get her.

"If being stuck in a ditch in the snow counts as okay, I'm fine," she replied, dredging up a sliver of wry humor.

"Where are you?" he asked quickly, his voice all business.

She told him where she was and bit back a sigh. Once again, Quinn would come to her rescue. Once again, he insisted she stay on the phone while he drove to find her.

"You keep making me do that. I'm not sure it's smart for you to drive while you're on the phone."

"It's on speaker," he countered. "Anyway, how the hell did you end up in a ditch?"

For a second, she considered glossing over what happened because her leg was already feeling more normal, the way it had the first time she got this weakness in it when they were hiking. But she didn't want to lie to him because even if she felt embarrassed and not too comfortable having to lean on him for help again, it went against her grain to try to pretend something else happened. She took a deep breath and rushed through her explanation.

He was quiet for a long moment, so long she got worried. "Now it's my turn to ask if you're there," she said into the silence.

"Right here. Trying not to worry too much and wondering why the hell you haven't been in to see Dr.

Marshall. You know, there are things that could help prevent these blips you're having."

She could hear the tightness in his voice and feel his concern straight through the phone line. Her heart set to banging inside her chest, hope drumming out its wishes with every beat. She forced herself to stay focused and gripped the phone tightly in her hand. Right now, the phone was her connection to Quinn and she was hanging on for dear life. "I know. I meant to get into see her, but I just haven't. I don't have any good excuses." She paused and took a breath, fighting the tears pressing hot against the back of her eyes. "I haven't been able to focus on much of anything except that I miss you. I miss you so much," she blurted out on a sob, her words escaping of their own volition.

He was dead silent for a moment, long enough for her to wish she could've kept her mouth shut.

"Hard to believe you miss me as much as I miss you," he finally said, his voice gruff.

Her heart soared and the tears she'd been holding at bay rolled freely down her cheeks. "I don't know," she said with a hiccup. "I've missed you an awful lot. This missing thing sucks."

His chuckle curled around her heart, easing its ache. "Damn right it does." The line crackled. "Hang on." His voice went in and out and then came through clear again. "Just rounded that curve on the hill where the reception disappears. I'm almost there."

Within a minute, she saw headlights on the road above the dip of the ditch. After another minute, she heard his footsteps through the snow and his face appeared at her window. She turned her car off and tucked the keys in her pocket. Quinn opened the door, and she almost burst into tears again. His eyes scanned her. When they landed back on her face, he leaned forward and caught her lips in a kiss.

Although it was a decidedly unromantic situation, one kiss from him and she almost melted right then and there. By the time he pulled back, her entire body was flexing toward him.

"Okay, we need to get you out of here."

He didn't even give her a chance to try to walk. He slipped an arm under her hips and carefully eased her into his arms. Once upon a time, she would have argued against this. Right now, it felt too good to be close to him. She relaxed into his hold and looped her arms around his shoulders.

* * *

QUINN SLOWLY CAME AWAKE and opened his eyes. It was still dark, but the moon shimmered outside and cast its light across the bed, limning Lacey's shoulder with a silvery glow. She was curled against him, her legs tangled with his. He took a deep breath and let it out slowly. Coming home with her had been a slice of heaven, while all that had happened was they'd had leftover pizza and watched television. He hadn't been up for much more talking, and she seemed to have been on the same wavelength. He'd insisted she call Dr. Marshall who had agreed it wasn't necessary for Lacey to come in since the weakness and tingling in her leg had resolved itself quickly this time. Lacey had scheduled the follow up appointment she'd been putting off for tomorrow. He rolled his head to glance at the clock on the nightstand— just past two in the morning, so no longer tomorrow, but today.

He closed his eyes, mentally replaying the moment when she'd told him she'd missed him. That's all he'd needed to hear to obliterate the temporary barriers he'd been trying to erect around his heart. He couldn't help but open his eyes again. He needed to see her. Even in the smudgy darkness of her bedroom with nothing but a dusting of light, she was so beautiful, his heart caught. He couldn't help but stroke his palm down her side, tracing the dip at her waist and the curve of her hip. Her skin was so soft. Funny, but until he'd been intimate with her, considering her soft in any way hadn't crossed his mind. She was all strength and verve, which had drawn him to her to begin with. Yet, now he was glad to know the softness she carried within. His body hummed, reminding him that he more than appreciated every inch of her soft curves, all the more tempting in contrast to her fit body.

Her breathing altered slightly and she shifted in her sleep, her leg sliding against his. His body tightened, his cock instantly hard. He was determined not to disturb her sleep, so he forced himself to breathe slowly and tried to get a grip on his body. When she moved again and mumbled something into his shoulder, he almost groaned aloud. She lifted her head, her hair a messy tousle around her face. Her eyes locked to his in the dimness. He held his breath, willing himself to keep his body under control. She lifted a hand and traced his lips. The coil of need tightened within him. He waited, barely breathing with his heart drumming and lust coursing through him.

Her fingertip traced down along his neck to follow the line of his collarbone and over his shoulder. Fire flashed in the wake of her feather light touch. Her eyes had followed her tracing, but they flicked back to his.

"I missed you," she whispered, her voice rough with sleep.

The raw vulnerability in her words struck at his heart. He brushed her hair away from her face and pushed up on one elbow. "Missed you too." He watched her as she blinked, almost as if she wasn't sure of his words. He threaded his hand into her hair and rose to meet her lips.

He'd show her just how much he missed her. He

captured her lips and tugged her closer. She didn't hesitate, half laying across his chest. The glide of her tongue against his sent the lust pounding through him in a wild beat. The air around them exploded with heat—their kiss as if oxygen to a fire. He poured weeks of longing into their kiss, stroking deeply into her mouth, savoring how she met him stroke for stroke. She tore her lips away and rose up to straddle him. He glanced up to see her silhouetted in the moonlight. Her hair fell in a tangle around her shoulders. Her breasts were outlined in the thin tank top she wore, her nipples taut against the fabric. He could feel her wet heat against his cock through her panties and his briefs. He couldn't stop from subtly lifting his hips and savored her gasp.

He slipped his hands under the hem of her tank top, slowly sliding them up, the fabric bunching as he pushed it up over her breasts. She caught it with one hand and flung it aside. Without waiting, he leaned forward and swirled his tongue around a nipple, rolling the other between his thumb and forefinger. A sharp cry broke from her as he switched his attention to her other breast, tracing damp circles on her skin where his mouth had been. Her breath came in broken gasps and breathy whimpers. Her hips rolled against him, tightening the need inside to the point he thought he might explode.

Suddenly, she shifted her hips back and tugged his briefs down. His cock sprang free, and she curled a hand around him, leaning forward to draw him in her mouth. His breath came out in a rough groan as he grappled to hang onto a thin thread of control. He was so close to the edge and so frantic for her, he could barely hold on as she dragged her tongue along the underside of his cock and took him fully in her mouth.

"Lace, come here..."

He barely managed to choke out the words. She rose, her

eyes pinned to him. He tugged her roughly forward, shoving the scrap of silk between her thighs out of the way and delving his fingers into her folds. She was so wet, he almost came at the feel of her. He dragged his fingers out and positioned his cock at her entrance. She didn't wait for him and lifted her hips slightly before sinking down on top of him, taking him deep inside of her. He looked up at her to find her eyes on him. Stroking a palm down her back, he eased her forward. With her breasts brushing against his chest, they slowly rocked together. He brushed a hand through her hair, his palm sliding down to cradle the side of her face. Her body started to ripple. She went taut and cried out, her channel convulsing around him, drawing his own release out—a long, slow arc of pleasure so intense, he shook to his core.

Lacey collapsed against him with her head falling to his shoulder as she curled into his arms. Stunned, he simply lay there as his heart gradually slowed and he could manage a breath. He idly sifted his fingers through her hair. She lifted her head, her eyes finding his in the dim light. The moonlight glimmered on her cheek, illuminating a tear. His chest tightened.

"Lace, are you okay?"

She nodded and took a breath. "More than okay. Maybe a little too good," she said, her voice raspy.

"Ah, well then I guess it's good to know I'm not alone."

A smile curled her lips and another tear rolled down her cheek, glittering in the moonlight. The moment felt so raw and intimate, his heart felt split wide open.

CHAPTER 20

*L*acey stood beside the kitchen counter and looked out over the field behind her cabin. Snow had blanketed the landscape during the night. She curled her hands around her coffee mug, savoring the warmth. A sip of the dark, delicious brew reminded her Quinn was here. Her efforts to match his coffee never met the mark. She heard footsteps on the stairs and turned to find him walking downstairs. He grinned, that easy grin she'd known for forever. She felt his smile right through to her toes. He walked straight to her and dipped his head to catch her lips in a quick kiss before stepping past her to pour his own cup of coffee.

The tiny moment sent flutters twirling through her, and her heart gave a little kick. A sense of pure relief washed through her. Quinn was here, with her, again. She slipped onto a stool beside the counter and watched while he poured maple syrup over the pancakes she'd made for him while he showered. He sat across from her and dug in. After several moments of sustained eating, he paused and glanced up.

"I was starving," he said, his mouth curling in another grin.

"I noticed," she replied, her own grin pretty much plastered on her face this morning.

"What time do you need to go into the office?"

His eyes flicked to the clock on the wall behind her. "First appointment at nine. I already texted Donna I might be a few minutes behind. I want to get the deck cleared of snow before I leave. I was thinking I could pull your car out of the ditch myself if you can wait until this afternoon. Up to you. Today's Donna's short day, so I'm free after noon." He paused, his eyes considering. When he spoke again, his tone was carefully neutral. "If you want me to go to your appointment with Dr. Marshall, I'd..."

"Please come with me," she said, jumping in. Over the last few weeks, her brain had nearly tied itself in knots, but one thing had become painfully clear. Quinn's support had held her together at times when she would've fallen apart in the last few months. She was done fighting against how much she wanted to allow herself to need him. She knew she could face all of this on her own, but she didn't want to push him away for the sake of proving that silly point. She wasn't sure how she'd incorporate this need into the relentlessly independent soul she'd defined herself as, but she would find a way.

His eyes widened at her abrupt interruption. After a moment, he nodded. "Okay then. How about I pick you up after I'm done at work? We'll go see Dr. Marshall and then deal with your car. Can you wait until this afternoon for your car?"

"Oh yeah. My office is home in the winter."

He nodded and eyed her again before taking a swallow of coffee. "Dr. Marshall's probably gonna want to talk to you about monitoring so you don't have another incident like yesterday."

The sense of anxiety threaded with panic that she'd felt on and off ever since she crashed to the ground in Katmai rose within. She took a breath and reminded herself she could manage this. She looked into his eyes and nodded. "I know. Maybe it seems like I was avoiding all this, but I guess I was trying to get used to it. There's that and then you."

"Me?"

"Yeah, you. I'm not used to relying on anyone other than myself." She shook her head. "That's true, but it's not what I mean right now. I'm not used to missing someone so much it hurt. I got all twisted up inside my brain because you were my friend and then, well, all kinds of stuff happened that I never expected." Her heart was beating wildly in her chest. She hadn't meant to say all this, but the words were tumbling out, as if frantic on their own to be heard. When she looked into his gaze, her anxiety eased. She slowly set her coffee cup on the counter and slipped off her stool to round the counter.

Without a word, he spun to meet her and pulled her close against him. She stood between his knees, tucked her head into his shoulder and just breathed him in. Standing in the shelter of his arms, she felt safe and protected. His heart beat, strong and steady, against her palm. She lifted her head to find his eyes waiting, tenderness, fire and understanding held within. He cleared his throat. "I love you, you know," he said.

She nodded, so overcome with emotion for a moment that she couldn't speak. He held her fast in his arms and in his gaze. After a gulp of air, she gathered herself. "I love you too. I don't know why I got all weird about us, but..." She lifted a shoulder in a shrug. "No need to worry about me being stupid about us again. It was awful without you. I don't ever want to go through that again," she said vehemently.

Quinn smiled softly, his eyes warm. "That's a good thing then because I'd put up a hell of a fight next time."

* * *

QUINN FOLLOWED Lacey out the door at Dr. Marshall's office and into the small parking lot. She held tight to his hand, while she gripped a folder of papers in another. Dr. Marshall had gotten her started on a course of medication to manage her relapses and decrease potential damage to her central nervous system. Dr. Marshall had also sent her away with various informational handouts on her medication and preventative monitoring. Lacey had been more relaxed and curious about what was happening than in any of the other times he'd been with her to the doctor. He chalked that up to the fact she wasn't coming after an event, no matter how minor, and she genuinely seemed to have come to terms with what she was facing.

As the last few weeks had unfolded, he'd come to realize that the woman he'd initially been attracted to—so strong, so bold and so full of life—was even more so now. It was different, yet somehow witnessing her let down her guard and let herself rely on anyone, much less him, was so humbling and brave, it only deepened the strength he so admired in her.

Later that evening, he leaned back against the couch and rolled his head to the side to look at Lacey. Her auburn hair fell forward as she leaned over to snag the remote off the coffee table. His heart gave a hard thump and lust coiled inside. It didn't seem to matter that just over an hour ago, he'd taken her roughly when she'd tugged him between her knees from where she'd been sitting on the kitchen counter. One kiss had set the low flames inside into a roaring burn, and they'd all but torn each other's clothes off. All she had to do was exist and he wanted her with a force he couldn't deny.

After pulling her car out of the ditch with his SUV and a handy towrope, he'd followed her back to her cabin earlier this evening. She'd insisted they have dinner at the lodge, so they'd tromped through the snowy trees for dinner with family and friends before returning.

A fire flickered behind the glass door of the woodstove. Lacey flicked through the channels and settled on the latest Alaskan reality show. She glanced over and grinned. "Let's see how realistic this one is. I swear, reality in reality shows is a bizarre thing."

He chuckled. "No worse for the Alaskan shows than the others."

She pushed a pillow out of the way between them and curled up against his side. He rested his arm across her shoulders and relaxed into the couch. They fell asleep like that. He woke during the night and looked around. Another snowstorm was blowing outside. Embers glowed in the woodstove. He carefully untangled himself from Lacey and slipped an arm under her hips to lift her as he stood. She mumbled something and lifted her head when he was about halfway up the stairs.

"What...? I can walk up the stairs, you know."

"I know, but I like to carry you."

She was quiet as he crested the landing at the top of the stairs and made his way to the bed. When he set her down, immediately laying down beside her and tucking the covers over them, she rolled over to face him and leaned up on an elbow. She lightly traced his brows.

"I didn't like it at first, but now I like it when you carry me," she said, her voice raspy in the darkness.

He stroked a hand through her hair and down her back as she relaxed against him.

EPILOGUE

*L*acey picked her way carefully along the trail, stepping around a boulder and jumping over a narrow stream winding its way through the backcountry. She and Quinn were leading another trip in Katmai National Park. It was almost a full year since they'd led the fated trip last year. Looking back now, she considered that trip a turning point in her life in more ways than one. She'd come a long way since she'd tried to dismiss the then-mysterious weakness and falls as random flukes. She'd been following Dr. Marshall's preventative treatment regimen down to the second and took precautions to have injections on hand when she traveled in the backcountry if she experienced any symptoms. She'd been in remission for her MS symptoms for over six months now and was mostly living life the way she had before, albeit with a heightened awareness of her health.

Beyond that, last year's trip to Katmai rung like a bell in her mind whenever she thought of it because it was then the spark was lit between her and Quinn. It may have taken a bit for her to get her head and heart on the same page, but once they were, there was no going back. Her life was one hundred percent with Quinn. They were still staying at the charming cabin on her parents' property, but they'd recently purchased some land on the other side of Last Frontier Lodge and were in the midst of overseeing the construction of their own home. For much of the summer, Quinn worked in his constantly busy practice, however he'd joined her on several of her longer backcountry trips and insisted he was coming on this one.

She glanced behind her to see him walking alongside one of their clients, Randy Martin, an elderly gentleman who'd become one of her regulars. Every summer, he signed up for a different trip with her company. Quinn was gesturing at the ground, so Lacey figured he was likely pointing out something to do with flora or fauna. She grinned and turned to face forward again.

Hours later, she stood at Quinn's side and looked out over a field of fireweed undulating under a chilly breeze. Fireweed was technically a weed, but it was the most spectacular weed Lacey had ever seen. Each year as summer wound down, massive fields of fireweed bloomed across Alaska. Bright, fuchsia flowers waved in the wind. They stood on a small viewing platform, which crossed a river adjacent to the field. Mountains rose in the distance on the far side of the fireweed. She leaned against the railing and glanced up at Quinn.

The sun had bronzed his chiseled features. His eyes canted to hers and his dangerously sexy grin curled his lips. Her heart skipped a beat and sent her pulse skittering wild. She wondered if that feeling would ever fade with him. Without thinking, she closed the distance between them and slipped her hand around his neck, tugging him down to meet her for a kiss. When she ran out of breath, she pulled back just as a gust of wind blew across the field and sent a shiver straight through her. He rubbed his hands up and down her arms. She could feel the heat of his touch through her thin jacket.

"Let's get inside. This jacket's fine when you're hiking, but you'll be freezing in no time if we keep standing here," he commented, curling one of his hands around hers and turning to walk toward the small cabin where they were staying.

This year, they'd rented a few cabins near the main park's buildings and viewing platforms at the famed Katmai River Falls. As they walked toward the cabin, they could see a few massive brown bears visible in the distance by the falls, patiently waiting to catch the salmon swimming through.

The following morning, Lacey enjoyed an actual shower. It was completely utilitarian, but a pure luxury in the backcountry. As she brushed her hair, the light caught on her ring. Months ago, Quinn had asked her to marry him, the moment both mundane and heart clenching. She'd just returned from a run on the beach with her hair a wild mess. He'd met her at the base of the path leading from the beach through the trees to her car. The second she saw the ring, a platinum band dotted with emeralds, she hadn't let him get a word out when she flung her arms around him.

She laughed to herself now and shook her head. They'd yet to plan a ceremony with their busy lives interfering. She finished getting dressed and stepped out of the cabin to find Quinn. Though it was summer, mornings in Katmai were cool. A refreshing breeze blew with the air so crisp and clean, it invigorated her with one breath. She strode towards the area where they'd set up camp for cooking and gathering when they weren't hiking and exploring. They'd only be here another day before they continued further on their trek and looped back to meet the plane and fly out.

When she reached the small clearing, she was startled to

find Marley and Gage there, along with her parents. Marley spun around, her face spreading in a grin.

"Hey! We actually surprised you," she said with glee.

Lacey walked to Marley who pulled her into a quick hug. Their mother joined them with their father holding back until Lacey broke away.

"Hey there," Stan said. "Bet you weren't expecting to see us here." He pulled her close for a quick hug and released her just as Quinn stepped into the clearing.

He grinned and came to her side. "So, by the look on your face, I actually pulled this off."

She looked up at him, her mind whirring with possibilities about his surprise. "You definitely surprised me, but I'm not sure what for."

"You said you'd marry me, but every time I tried to ask about planning it, you kept saying we had too much going on. So...I planned it myself. I figured you wouldn't want anything fancy, but you just might like getting married out where you love to be. I persuaded your family to fly out here. My mom and Amelia will be here in another hour or so. In case you didn't know it, Randy is an ordained minister. He's agreed to marry us."

Lacey's mouth fell open. She finally managed to shut it, while a wild sense of joy flooded her. When she didn't say anything for a few moments too long, Quinn spoke again.

"Is this okay?" he asked, his amber eyes warm and concerned.

She nodded and swiped at the tears welling. Her family, seeming to get a clue, dispersed, leaving her and Quinn alone in the small clearing. He stepped to her and reached for her hands. "Are you sure? If you're having second thoughts..."

She shook her head sharply and flung herself against him, wrapping her arms tightly around his shoulders and tucking her head into his neck. "No second thoughts. None at all," she finally said, lifting her head and leaning back to look at him.

He grinned. "I love you, you know."

"I know, I know." She placed her hand over his heart, feeling the strong, steady beat. "I love you too. I can't believe you pulled this off."

* * *

QUINN LOOKED across at Lacey as Randy finished pronouncing them officially bound for life and his breath caught. Their marriage ceremony had been as simple as it gets with the wilderness they both loved providing a grand and spectacular setting. He gave her hands a small tug as he stepped to her and caught her lips in a kiss. As usual, he completely forgot everything the moment her lips touched his and broke away with a laugh when Marley cheered.

Their 'reception' consisted of a remarkably good meal organized by their respective families with quite a bit of help from the rangers and other visitors in the remote park. Hours later, Quinn walked hand in hand with Lacey through the falling darkness toward their tiny cabin. They walked across the viewing platform where she gave his hand a pull and turned to lean against the railing. The moon sat low above the mountains in the dusky light, illuminating the jagged peaks against the darkening sky. He slipped his arms around her waist from behind and rested his head in the curve of her neck. He took a deep breath, luxuriating in the scent and feel of her in his arms. She angled her head back against his shoulder.

"Today was amazing," she whispered, her words clear in the crisp night air.

"You amaze me every day. Let's keep it that way." His words came out rough, his heart so full, he could barely breathe.

He dipped his head and dropped a kiss on her neck. She spun in his arms and cupped his face in her hands. "With you, amazing is easy."

Thank you for reading When We Fall - I hope you loved Lacey & Quinn's story!

This Crazy Love kicks off my new series, the Swoon Series - small town southern romance with enough heat to melt you! Jackson & Shay's story is epic - steamy & intensely emotional. Jackson just happens to be Shay's brother's best friend. He's also *seriously* easy on the eyes. Shay has a past, the kind of past she would most definitely like to forget. Past or not, Jackson is about to rock her world. Don't miss their story!

For more swoony & sassy romance, check out my website for the following stories: https://jhcroixauthor.com/books/

This Crazy Love kicks off the Swoon Series - small town southern romance with enough heat to melt you! Jackson & Shay's story is epic - swoon-worthy & intensely emotional. Jackson just happens to be Shay's brother's best friend. He's also *seriously* easy on the eyes. Shay has a past, the kind of past she would most definitely like to forget. Past or not, Jackson is about to rock her world. Don't miss their story! Free on all retailers!

Burn For Me is a second chance romance for the ages. Sexy firefighters? Check. Rugged men? Check. Wrapped up together? Check. Brave the fire in this hot, small-town romance. Amelia & Cade were high school sweethearts & then it all fell apart. When they cross paths again, it's epic - don't miss Cade's story!

Free on all retailers!

For more small town romance, take a visit to Last Frontier Lodge in Diamond Creek. A sexy, alpha SEAL meets his match with a brainy heroine in Take Me Home. Marley is all brains & Gage is all brawn. Sparks fly when their worlds collide. Don't miss Gage & Marley's story!
Free on all retailers!

If sports romance lights your spark, check out The Play. Liam is a British footballer who falls for Olivia, his doctor. A twist of forbidden heats up this swoon-worthy & laugh-out-loud romance. Don't miss Liam & Olivia's story.
Free on all retailers!

Sign up for my newsletter, so you can receive information about upcoming new releases & receive a FREE copy of one of my books: http://jhcroixauthor.com/subscribe/

Thank you for reading When We Fall! I hope you enjoyed the story. If so, you can help other readers find my books in a variety of ways.

1) Write a review!
2) Sign up for my newsletter, so you can receive information about upcoming new releases & receive a FREE copy of one of my books: http://jhcroixauthor.com/subscribe/
3) Like and follow my Amazon Author page at https://amazon.com/author/jhcroix
4) Follow me on Bookbub at https://www.bookbub.com/authors/j-h-croix
5) Follow me on Instagram at https://www.instagram.com/jhcroix/
6) Like my Facebook page at https://www.facebook.com/jhcroix

* * *

Last Frontier Lodge Novels
Take Me Home
Love at Last
Just This Once
Falling Fast
Stay With Me
When We Fall
Hold Me Close
Crazy For You
Just Us
Dare With Me Series
Crash Into You
Evers & Afters
Come To Me
Back To Us
Swoon Series
This Crazy Love
Wait For Me
Break My Fall
Truly Madly Mine
Still Go Crazy
If We Dare
Steal My Heart
Into The Fire Series
Burn For Me
Slow Burn
Burn So Bad
Hot Mess
Burn So Good
Sweet Fire
Play With Fire
Melt With You
Burn For You
Crash & Burn
That Snowy Night

Brit Boys Sports Romance

The Play

Big Win

Out Of Bounds

Play Me

Naughty Wish

Diamond Creek Alaska Novels

When Love Comes

Follow Love

Love Unbroken

Love Untamed

Tumble Into Love

Christmas Nights

ACKNOWLEDGMENTS

To friends near and dear to my heart who inspired Lacey's story. Always…my hubby who makes sure I keep my sanity while writing like mad and who reminds me every day what's important in life. My editor continues to ruthlessly remind me what each story needs to make it better than it began and then some. Najla Qamber takes my ideas and creates stunning covers. Most importantly: my readers… thank you from the bottom of my heart for your enthusiasm and for cheering for the next book over and over again!

xoxo

J.H. Croix

ABOUT THE AUTHOR

USA Today Bestselling Author J. H. Croix lives in a small town in the historical farmlands of Maine with her husband and two spoiled dogs. Croix writes contemporary romance with sassy women and alpha men who aren't afraid to show some emotion. Her love for quirky small-towns and the characters that inhabit them shines through in her writing. Take a walk on the wild side of romance with her best-selling novels!

Places you can find me:
jhcroixauthor.com
jhcroix@jhcroix.com